W9-AQA-528

Praise for DAME AGATHA'S SHORTS

"Agatha Christie was nearly as famous for her short stories as she was for her novels, and Elena Santangelo has compiled the most readable guide and in-depth companion to Agatha's Shorts that any fan could ever wish for. No mystery library, personal or public, should be without this resource. Elena Santangelo has created a gem, enhanced by her own thorough knowledge of writing short stories and her love of the genre."

—Charles Todd, author of A Matter of Justice and A Duty to the Dead

"Dame Agatha's Shorts is a delicious romp through Christie's life and stories. A must-read for Christie lovers, and a superior reference book for those who crave details. Santangelo weaves together a wealth of information, making it both enjoyable and educational."

—Judy Clemens, author of the Anthony- and Agatha-nominated Stella Crown series

"For Christie fans, DAME AGATHA'S SHORTS, is the answer to a prayer. Santangelo provides the first source book of Agatha Christie's short fiction in easy prose, with a dash of humor. Her enthusiasm for the Dame's stories is contagious. Readers of this book will want to drop everything and take off on an anthology hunt. And I will be leading the pack!"

—Robin Hathaway, author of Sleight of Hand

Dame,
Agatha's
Shorts

Dame, Agatha's Shorts

An Agatha Christie Short Story Companion

ELENA SANTANGELO

HA CASS COUNTY PUBLIC LIBRARY
400 E. MECHANIC
HARRISONVILLE, MO 64701

0 0022 0567208 8

BellaRosaBooks

Dame Agatha's Shorts
ISBN 978-1-933523-72-9

Copyright © 2009 Elena Santangelo

Agatha Christie quotes and cover photograph:
Copyright © The Estate of Agatha Christie.

All rights reserved, including the right to reproduce this
book or portions thereof in any form whatsoever.
For more information contact
Bella Rosa Books, P.O. Box 4251 CRS, Rock Hill, SC 29732.
Or online at www.bellarosabooks.com

First Printing: May 2009

Library of Congress Control Number: 2009926668

Printed in the United States of America on acid-free paper.

Book design by Bella Rosa Books

BellaRosaBooks and logo are trademarks of Bella Rosa Books

10   9   8   7   6   5   4   3   2   1

Table of Contents

Foreword

As a child, whenever I grew bored with my own books, I would sneak into my brother's room and forage through his bookshelves. In this way, I was introduced to Encyclopedia Brown, the Hardy Boys, and Donald Sobol's Two Minute Mysteries.

Seeing a trend in my pillaging, my brother gave me two Agatha Christie novels: Mrs. McGinty's Dead and The Murder of Roger Ackroyd. After that, I hit the bookstores in search of every Christie title I could find. And not far into this process, I brought home The Regatta Mystery.

When I realized the book wasn't a novel but a collection of short stories, I was disappointed. I wanted a nice long read, something meaty that I could sink my brain into. Then I began reading. The stories were incredibly well-crafted—but of course, I didn't realize this until I became a writer myself. I simply knew how much I enjoyed reading them. When I finished "In A Glass Darkly," the eerie mood and amazing ending stayed with me for days. Not long after, I added Witness for the Prosecution—Christie's finest short story anthology—to my collection. At that point, I was hooked.

Every mystery fan I've met has at least heard of Christie's novels, but very few readers seem to realize that Dame Agatha not only wrote short stories (more than 160 of them!), but that she was a master of the short form.

Bedside companion books examining Christie's writings have usually concentrated on the novels, at best giving the story collections a brief mention, and rarely discussing individual tales. They can't be blamed. She produced so many works in her lifetime that no one volume could possibly do them all justice.

And so, that we might see and appreciate the flowers in the forest, I'm going to remove the trees. This book will deal exclusively with the short stories. A novel or play may be mentioned here and there, but only those expanded from or directly related to the shorts.

If you're exploring Dame Agatha's short fiction for the first time, or looking for tales you may have missed, or perhaps taking a second or third read through them all, I hope this book will be a helpful companion. If you're a writer, I encourage you to examine the craft in Christie's short stories. You can't ask for a better mentor.

Enjoy!
Elena Santangelo

Author's Notes

All quotes attributed to Christie in this book were taken from An Autobiography, Agatha Christie, Ballantine Books, New York, 1977.

Most of Christie's stories were published in periodicals first, and where I know details, I've listed original publication and date with each title.

Since most of the anthologies are titled after a short story, I've used the following conventions to help eliminate confusion: short stories are in quotes, periodicals and plays are in italics, and novels and anthologies are underlined.

Within the confines of these covers, I define "mystery" as a story with a puzzle that needs solving or element that needs revealing. However, a "detective story" is where a main character actually engages in some sort of detection. With the exception of Poirot, almost all of Christie's detectives are amateurs or act as amateurs.

Chapter 1

Murder Through the Years

A QUICK TIMELINE

Agatha Christie's publishing career stretched nearly six decades, so perhaps the quantity of her short stories doesn't seem surprising. An average of three stories a year. How hard could that be? But nearly a hundred were published before the end of the 1920s (and many of these were written before World War I). Only a handful were written later than 1950.

The 1920s

This decade should have been a wonderful time for Christie. After all, her first novel, The Mysterious Affair at Styles, saw print in 1920, and by 1926, after the publication of her sixth novel, The Murder of Roger Ackroyd, she'd attained fame and a small independent income as a mystery author.

Her private life, though, was filled with stress and unpleasantness. Her mother died not long after Roger Ackroyd came out, and Christie admitted that she wanted nothing more than to wallow in her own sorrow. Her husband, Archie, whom Christie described as "having a violent dislike of illness, death and trouble of any kind" hated being around her while she was grieving. Christie went to her mother's house to clean it and close the estate. Only her daughter Rosalind went with her. Archie refused to come down even for an occasional weekend. Christie became very depressed, then so confused and muddled that she tells of one episode where she was writing a check and couldn't remember what name to sign. She cried for no reason and ate less and less.

When Archie finally did come to see his wife, he told her he'd met another woman and wanted a divorce. In 1928, the marriage officially ended and Christie was left as a single mother with a daughter to raise and a house to maintain. Suddenly mystery writing became her only way to make a living.

Penning short stories in addition to novels helped. Up through the early 1930s, many periodicals published fiction in serial form. Magazines like *The Sketch* would buy six short stories at a time, usually all with the same detective. Plenty of work existed for any good writer who wanted it.

> "The nice part about writing in those days was that I directly related it to money. If I decided to write a story, I knew it would bring me in sixty pounds, or whatever. . . . This stimulated my output enormously."

She may have had a mercenary outlook, but the desire to produce a saleable product didn't drive her to write by a set formula. Within those early years, in her short stories alone, she experimented with no less than five series detectives (counting Tuppence and Tommy Beresford as one, since they were a sleuthing team). Christie also invented several supporting characters who would return in later novels. At least thirty of her early stories had no series character at all, and quite a few of them weren't even mysteries. For the sake of analysis, I've labeled these non-mysteries supernatural or romance.

Christie's supernatural tales explore the unexplained and eerie things around us and within us. She tackled the human side of the occult. Christie had a true gift for conjuring these plots. Some of her best stories fall into this genre.

When I say "romance," I use the broadest definition. These stories are about relationships, usually love, though not always. Some are dark, brooding psychological studies, some tragedies, and some happy, lighthearted romps.

The 1930s
"Those years, between 1930 and 1938, were particularly satisfying because they were so free of outside shadows."

She met and became happily married to archaeologist Max Mallowan, helping him with his work by taking up photography and traveling with him to the Middle East. Earning money with short stories became less necessary. About the same time, she found a new writing toy: plays.

"I should always write my one book a year—I was sure of that. Dramatic writing would be my adventure . . ."

Still, in the short story collections that came out of this decade, especially in the last five years, we see a new confidence in her writing. Most of the stories were mysteries, most featuring her impish little Belgian detective, Hercule Poirot, but she began experimenting with the novelette form, and with the short story as plot sketch. She later expanded many shorts of this period into novels.

The 1940s
World War II came to England. In her autobiography, Christie speaks of having bombs come down all around her house in London:

"I became used in the end to raids on London—so much so that I hardly woke up. I would think, half drowsily, that I heard the siren, or bombs not too far away."

She had a fear of being buried underground, and so never went to the air raid shelters. One weekend when she and Max were away from London, a bomb fell directly across the street from her home, leveling three houses and damaging her roof, top floor, and basement. "My Steinway was never quite the same afterwards," she wrote, and she finally moved, mainly because she now had to use a ladder to get to her front door.

During the war years, she worked about four days a week at a local hospital. She also produced fourteen mystery novels. She'd begun a practice of working on two books simultaneously, so if writer's block hit with one, she could concentrate on the other. Of the fourteen, she wrote two to be published after her death, which she thought might be imminent, given the bombs dropping in her front yard. These two were her final Poirot and Miss Marple cases: <u>Curtain</u> and <u>Sleeping Murder</u> respectively.

Besides the mysteries, she worked on two romantic novels, three plays, and an autobiography about travels with Max in Syria. Many sources cite the wartime works as Christie's very finest writing.

> "I produced an *incredible* amount of stuff during those years: I suppose it was because there were no distractions of a social nature; one practically never went out in the evenings."

However, the war was a dry period for short stories. The markets for shorts were much less plentiful by that time, especially in England.

The first twelve shorts that she wrote after the war were Poirot stories, but with a huge difference. The development in writing style and characterization between these tales and those of the previous decade can only be described as dramatic. The plots are ingenious, the storytelling three-dimensional. The moods aren't as light as the 1920s mysteries, nor as overly serious as the 1930s works. Every aspect is balanced and consistent.

The 1950s, 60s and 70s

". . . it was no longer really worthwhile for me to work so hard: one book a year was ample. If I wrote two books a year I should make hardly more than by writing one, and only give myself a great deal of extra work."

Rampant taxation and an easier home life gave Christie reasons to slow down in later years. She could devote herself to projects she wanted to do, for instance, writing a radio play for the Queen Mother's birthday. Later that little twenty minute play would be rewritten as a short story, then as the full-length drama, *The Mousetrap*.

Several of her shorts of this period developed in the same fashion, as sketches for longer plays and novels. In some ways, these are the most novel-like of all her short stories.

Yet, as she stated above, she no longer felt a need to work hard. If she saw a second annual novel as an unprofitable venture, short stories had become downright charity. Most, if not all, of the stories to appear in these scarce last collections were actually written, and some published, in the twenties and thirties. Most are not her best work. However, a few do stand out: "Three Blind Mice" and "The Dressmaker's Doll" are two of my favorites. They will be discussed in later chapters.

So, six decades of short stories. Where to begin? In the place most readers will find these stories: the anthologies.

Chapter 2
One and Twenty Anthologies . . . and Other Stories

The vast majority of Christie short stories were first printed in periodicals, many in series of four to six at a time. Every few years these stories would be compiled into a Christie-only anthology. Twenty such collections were published during her lifetime.

Here is an overview of these anthologies. In the listing below, if the English and American titles differ, I list the English one first, followed by the American title.

1924 POIROT INVESTIGATES

Like her first novel, Christie's first stories to make it into print featured her most famous detective, as narrated by his faithful sidekick, Captain Hastings. All fourteen of the stories in this collection were published in *The Sketch* in 1923.

These tales very much show the influence of Conan Doyle's Sherlock Holmes. Hastings talks of recording Poirot's cases the way Watson talks of penning Holmes' investigations. The titles, most of which begin with "The Adventure of . . .", are also suggestive of Holmes.

The collection and its stories will be discussed in detail in chapter 4.

1927 THE BIG FOUR

Twelve Poirot short stories are linked with a rather heavy-handed main plot concerning master criminals out to rule the world. The result is a kind of unnatural mutation between novel and short story collection. Most of the tales in The Big Four are more like chapters than finished shorts. The stories must be read in order. All were first published in The Sketch early in 1924.

1929 PARTNERS IN CRIME

Like The Big Four, this is another linked collection, but beautifully done. Tuppence and Tommy Beresford take on the running of a detective agency (the how and why are discussed in chapter 5), which enables them to try out the methods of all their favorite fictional detectives. This is the funniest set of stories Christie ever wrote. Most were published in The Sketch late in 1924 and, sadly, are the only Tuppence and Tommy shorts, fourteen in all.

1930 THE MYSTERIOUS MR. QUIN

Here are twelve excellent tales featuring Harley Quin, a supernatural protagonist based on the harlequin character of early plays (portrayed sometimes as unearthly clown, sometimes as demon). Mr. Quin is also Christie's first series character to appear only in short stories. Mr. Satterthwaite is Mr. Quin's "Watson" and his link to the mortal world. Nine of these stories are solid mysteries. Of the other three, two are more like romances, and the last, more of a supernatural tale. See chapter 6 for more on this collection.

1932 THIRTEEN PROBLEMS / THE TUESDAY
CLUB MURDERS

Miss Jane Marple made her debut in two series of six stories before Murder at the Vicarage appeared in 1930. The series are linked only by the setting where each narrator relates them—dinner parties with Miss Marple in attendance. For this collection, one last unrelated story was added to make thirteen (hence the English title), Christie's first of many anthologies to use that magic number of tales.

This is also Miss Marple's only original solo collection. Other Miss Marple stories shared anthology space with Poirot, Parker Pyne and other stories. The later Miss Marple collections contain only reprints that first appeared in these earlier collections.

1933 THE HOUND OF DEATH AND OTHER STORIES

The majority of the tales in this English collection are either supernatural, or mysteries with supernatural elements. This was the first collection of her works that didn't feature a single protagonist throughout, and the first collection to feature non-Quin supernatural tales, though many of the stories were first printed in periodicals up to ten years earlier. Five of the stories are mysteries, though none with a series detective. Hound of Death was the first anthology to carry "Witness for the Prosecution," perhaps her most famous short.

1934 THE LISTERDALE MYSTERY

This British collection contains all mysteries that have no series detectives (and a few have no detective at all). The stories show a wonderfully wide variety of settings, characters, and moods. Some of Christie's finest shorts were first anthologized in this book. "Philomel Cottage" and "Accident" went on to appear in more anthologies than any other of her stories.

1934 PARKER PYNE INVESTIGATES / MR. PARKER PYNE: DETECTIVE

These twelve tales feature Parker Pyne, a retired government statistician who opens an agency—not a detective agency, mind you, but a firm that seeks to make people happy. Despite both titles, Mr. Pyne's occupation, at least in the earliest stories, is primarily that of busybody. A charming character. Miss Lemon (secretary-extraordinaire) and Mrs. Ariadne Oliver (Christie's parody of herself) both make their debuts in this book.

1937 MURDER IN THE MEWS / DEAD MAN'S MIRROR

An anthology of four Poirot novelettes. I've included them with her short stories simply because they aren't discussed much otherwise, but in form, they're closer to novels than short stories. According to some references, "The Incredible Theft" was missing from the American version, but my Bantam paperback (the 1984 printing) does include the story, so this was remedied at some point. The only difference in the American and English versions seems to be the order of the contents, each beginning with its respective title story.

1939 THE REGATTA MYSTERY

This collection was originally published in the United States only, with no comparable United Kingdom anthology. The book contains two Parker Pyne stories, a Miss Marple tale, and one jaunt into the supernatural, but Poirot is the favored son here, with five stories. The Regatta Mystery is another fine collection.

1947 THE LABOURS OF HERCULES

Christie's first anthology of linked stories since Partners in Crime. The collection might well be sub-titled "Poirot's Last Cases" not only because he claims he'll retire when they're all solved, but because the only two Poirot stories to be published after them are retellings of earlier tales. The Labours of Hercules, in my opinion, is the best overall collection of Poirot shorts.

1948 WITNESS FOR THE PROSECUTION

This American collection has been called the finest single grouping of Christie's short stories. If you're looking to read your first Christie short, I'd recommend starting with Witness for the Prosecution. Every story in it is an excellent read.

That said, it contains only one series detective mystery, starring Poirot. One supernatural tale is also included. The remaining seven stories are non-series mysteries. Except for the Poirot short, all the others appeared earlier in either The Hound of Death or The Listerdale Mystery anthologies in the 1930s.

1950 THREE BLIND MICE AND OTHER STORIES

This American anthology has also been titled The Mousetrap and Other Stories. The title story is a novelette based on Christie's play, *The Mousetrap* (discussed in chapter 9). Otherwise, you'll find four Miss Marple stories from the 1940s, one 1926 Mr. Quin tale, and three Poirot stories from 1923, 1929, and 1940.

1951 THE UNDER DOG AND OTHER MYSTERIES

In this single-detective collection featuring Poirot, eight of the nine stories were among Christie's first published shorts, printed in *The Sketch* in 1923. The title story isn't much younger, having appeared in *London Magazine* in 1926. See chapter 4 for more details on this anthology and its stories.

1960 THE ADVENTURE OF THE CHRISTMAS PUDDING

I have to wonder why this English collection wasn't an all-Poirot anthology. Of the six stories, five feature the little Belgian. The sixth, however, is a Miss Marple tale. All of the contents except the title story appeared in previous collections. Oddly enough, Christie rewrote the title story that same year, turning it into "The Theft of the Royal Ruby," for inclusion in Double Sin and Other Stories (see below).

1961 DOUBLE SIN AND OTHER STORIES

This American anthology was published in 1961. Of the eight stories in this collection, four feature Poirot, two Miss Marple, and two fall into the supernatural genre.

1961 13 FOR LUCK!
Here is a collection of mystery stories for young readers, containing all of Christie's series sleuths except the Beresfords, plus the non-series mystery "Accident." All of these stories appeared in previous collections.

1965 SURPRISE! SURPRISE!
The same Christie's series detectives as in 13 For Luck! are also represented in this volume of tales with surprise endings. These stories all appeared in previous collections.

1966 13 CLUES FOR MISS MARPLE
Thirteen of Miss Marple's twenty shorts are gathered here into one collection. All of these tales appeared in previous collections.

1971 THE GOLDEN BALL AND OTHER STORIES
Towards the end of Christie's life, American readers were at last given an anthology containing the rest of the stories from The Hound of Death and The Listerdale Mystery. This combined non-series mysteries with supernatural tales, and added two not-yet-anthologized stories, both romances. A delightful collection.

1974 HERCULE POIROT'S EARLY CASES
This American collection of Poirot stories was first published between 1923 and 1935. All of the tales appeared in previous anthologies.

Many anthologies including Christie short stories have been printed since her death—too many to list them all here. Still, the publishers of those collections should be commended for doing their part toward keeping Christie's shorts accessible to the reading public. I will mention one, however, because some of the stories in it are difficult to find otherwise:

1989 THE HARLEQUIN TEA SET

Although this anthology was published thirteen years after Christie's death, I list it here because all but two of the tales had never previously appeared in any other collection, only in periodicals. The first magazine printings and dates are listed on the copyright page, making it possible to read the works in the order of publication.

The Harlequin Tea Set is one of the best sources for the earliest non-mysteries. They are, in some ways, those stories that didn't make the cut for The Hound of Death anthology, but the reader can get a feel for what was going on in Christie's mind during those first years of writing. Included is her very first short story, mentioned in her autobiography, "House of Dreams."

Chapter 3

The Case of the Fortuitous Germ

THE EARLIEST SHORTS

Influenza killed millions of people worldwide in the first two decades of the twentieth century. Fortunately, Agatha Miller (Christie's maiden name) wasn't one of them. In her auto-biography, though, she does tell of coming down with the virus when she was about twelve years old. She must have had a nasty case of the bug, because her recovery was lengthy.

About being stuck in bed, she wrote, "I was bored. I had read lots of books . . . and was now reduced to dealing myself bridge hands." Her mother suggested she write a story.

At first Christie didn't think she could. She'd written some poetry, but never anything like a story. Still, she had nothing else to do, so she gave it a try. "It was exhausting, and did not assist my convalescence, but it was exciting, too."

Only a day or two later, "House of Beauty" was completed.

"Amateurishly written" Christie said of it years later, "showing the influence of all that I had read the week before. . . . Just then I had obviously been reading D. H. Lawrence." Yet she also wrote, ". . . the first thing I ever wrote that showed any sign of promise." Few writers can say that of their first stories, let alone of anything written at age twelve.

Other tales followed: "The Call of Wings," "The Lonely God," and ". . . a grisly story about a séance," which later became "The Last Séance." Following her mother's advice, she typed them all up on her sister's Empire typewriter, then sent them off to various magazines under the pseudonym Mack Miller.

"I had not much hope of success," she recalls, and sure enough, all the stories were returned with standard rejection slips. She rewrapped them, sent them off to other magazines, over and over, eventually changing her pseudonym to Nathaniel Miller (her grandfather's name). She wrote more stories, typed them, and sent them off as well.

She began reading the works of May Sinclair, who was to Christie "one of our finest and most original novelists." A Sinclair short story called "The Flaw in the Crystal" so caught Christie's imagination that she wrote one in the same vein which she titled "Vision." (More discussion of this story can be found in chapter 10.)

The rejections still came, but she kept at it. "I'd formed a habit of writing stories by this time. It took the place, shall we say, of embroidering cushion covers. . . ."

All of these early stories were eventually rewritten and published in the 1920s and early 30s. None of these first works were mysteries. Most were tales of the supernatural ("I was addicted to writing psychic stories . . ."), with a few romances thrown in.

Christie's first four stories are listed below in the order written, according to her autobiography (An Autobiography, Ballantine Books, 1977).

"House of Dreams"
—*Sovereign Magazine*, January 1926

This is Christie's first story, originally titled "House of Beauty."

As she said, she was reading D. H. Lawrence at the time, though the flu probably also made her mind run to morose and supernatural topics. The story explores insanity, death, and immortality.

"House of Dreams" reads like a first story. The third person narrative sounds very young and the dialogue between the teenaged girls is exactly the right timbre of youth and unsophistication. Yet when you remember that Christie was even younger than her characters, the tale does indeed "show promise" of what was to come!

Although "House of Dreams" was first published in *Sovereign Magazine* in 1926, it didn't appear in a short story collection until The Harlequin Tea Set (1989).

"The Call of Wings"
—The Hound of Death, 1933

This was written soon after "House of Dreams" and, in theme, is much like it, with an added parable quality: After a rich man hears the "wings," he's only happy when shedding his possessions. (Christie admitted that she tended to moralize in her early stories). As far as I can tell, it wasn't published in a periodical before appearing in The Hound of Death anthology.

"The Lonely God"
—*Royal Magazine*, July 1926

Written about the same time as "Call of Wings," this has only a tiny hint of the unexplained in it, which enhances the plot, but doesn't drive it. Instead, "Lonely God" is a romance about the psychology of loneliness. It's less complicated than her supernatural tales, with a simple plot that holds together well. Christie claims she'd read something "regrettably sentimental" just before writing it. However, the story is a gem, saved from being commonplace by the character of a little stone god. Look for it in The Harlequin Tea Set.

"The Last Séance"
—unknown, 1926

A medium performs one last séance before retiring, failing to take into account the needs of her client. Written about the same time as the two above, this story is also completely different in character, as if Christie were trying on a variety of hats. "Grisly" is indeed the best description. This is her first Poe-like horror story, and was included in The Hound of Death collection, 1933. Since the copyright is 1926, the story was likely published in a periodical first, though sources are vague as to that point.

Many other stories were published in the early 1920s as well. These will be discussed in subsequent chapters, according to sleuth and genre.

Chapter 4

The Adventures of Hercule Poirot

"Madge had initiated me young on Sherlock Holmes," Christie said of her and her sister's love of detective stories. Even before little Agatha could read them, Madge would recount plots such as <u>The Leavenworth Case</u> to her. By the time Agatha was seventeen, they were reading the Arsene Lupin stories and <u>The Mystery of the Yellow Room</u>, then discussing them afterward.

Not long after that, Christie mentioned to her sister that someday she'd like to try writing a detective story.

" 'I bet you couldn't,' " said her sister.

Sibling dares are the best motivators. The notion stayed in the back of Christie's mind until World War I. As she was writing her supernatural and romantic stories, she was also taking mental notes about her work in a hospital dispensary, and about the Belgian refugees that came to England.

Her first mystery tale was a novel: <u>The Mysterious Affair at Styles</u> featuring detective Hercule Poirot. Still, she was already comfortable with the short story form, so Poirot short mysteries soon began to flow from her typewriter. In fact, these may have been the first Christie shorts to be published.

In her lifetime, Christie wrote more than fifty Poirot shorts (about one third of her total short story output). Nearly half of them first appeared in periodicals in 1923.

POIROT INVESTIGATES (1924)

As stated in chapter 2, the early stories in Poirot Investigates showed the influence of Conan Doyle, and also Christie's love of parody. The narrative style is sometimes Watson-like, except that Captain Hastings reveals his emotions more, especially when he's angry at Poirot for making him look like a fool. Much to Hastings' chagrin, Poirot refuses to be anything like Holmes.

Many of the stories in Poirot Investigates suffer from a sameness, as if Christie were trying to work out a formula for her mystery shorts. They are, in a way, her student works, and should be read as such. Interestingly enough, the first batch of these stories to be published were the least formula-driven. In many of them, Hastings assumes a character of his own instead of pretending to be Dr. Watson. I suspect this is a result of the 1923 editor at *The Sketch* choosing the best first, then, after Christie became popular, taking stories with more formula, which may have been written earlier.

In all the tales, Poirot is infused with energy, though he speaks of sitting still and letting his brain do the work. His character is fresh and spirited, and a terrific contrast to Hastings who is at his stuffiest.

I present them in the order they appear in the collection, because they to seem flow better that way than chronologically by publication date (which is listed below each title).

"The Adventure of 'The Western Star' "
—*The Sketch*, April 1923

Compare the opening of this story with Conan Doyle's "The Adventure of the Beryl Coronet." Enough similarities exist that the reader has to wonder what Christie was up to. This is no simple copy, though, but more of a parody, as if Hastings was assigning himself Watson's role, only to have Poirot ruin the mood by not playing along the way he's supposed to.

In the story, "The Western Star" is a fabulous diamond, destined to meet its mate, "The Star of the East." This is Christie's first "big jewel" story. She would return to this theme many times in years to come.

Inspector Japp makes his debut, but only as a mention in the middle and a walk-on at the end.

"The Tragedy at Marsdon Manor"
—*The Sketch*, May 1923

Poirot is commissioned by an insurance company to investigate the death of a man who recently insured his life for fifty thousand pounds. For a young writer, this story has a very graceful flow between scenes. She changes locations adroitly, in one or two sentences. No seams. Novelists who attempt the short story form for the first time would do well to study it.

"The Adventure of the Cheap Flat"
—*The Sketch*, May 1923

Friends of Hastings find a flat in a fashionable neighborhood, and at a dirt cheap rate. This theme also recurs—see "The Listerdale Mystery" (discussed in chapter 9). Poirot decides to investigate the cheapness of the flat. "Poirot, you're not serious!" Hastings exclaims, but the little Belgian is, and sure enough, he discovers a crime. The final explanation's perhaps a little too farfetched to believe, but the story is charming and full of action. Also published under "Poirot Indulges a Whim."

"The Mystery of Hunter's Lodge"
—*The Sketch*, May 1923

This story has a much more Christie-like beginning, in which she harks back to her own bout of influenza. Poirot has the virus, so Hastings goes off to investigate a murder on his own. The setting though—in the middle of the moors—is reminiscent of <u>The Hound of the Baskervilles</u>.

"The Million Dollar Bond Robbery"
—*The Sketch*, May 1923

A million dollars in Liberty Bonds disappear from the ocean liner *Olympia*, en route from London to New York. " 'Me, I always know when I am on the sea,' said Poirot sadly." And so we're introduced to his lifelong aversion to traveling by ship. The mystery plot is tantalizing, though a few facts are withheld from the reader. They may not be necessary to solve the puzzle, but I felt slightly cheated in the end.

"The Adventure of the Egyptian Tomb"
—*The Sketch*, September, 1923

The men present at the opening of a newly discovered Egyptian tomb begin to die, all of different causes. In this story, again, Hastings attempts to mimic Watson in his early narration, but what Poirot must endure in traveling to Egypt is too funny for this one to remain Holmes-like for long.

"The Jewel Robbery at the Grand Metropolitan"
—*The Sketch*, March 1923

Hastings and Poirot travel to Brighton for a vacation weekend, but the theft of an expensive necklace makes it a busman's holiday. Nothing really Holmes-ish about this one, as if Christie also took a holiday from that style. Originally published under the title "The Curious Disappearance of the Opalsen Pearls."

"The Kidnapped Prime Minister"
—*The Sketch*, April 1923

A World War I mystery in which England's prime minister disappears just before an important conference in France. Here Hastings' narrative takes on a life of its own. This feels like more of an "adventure" story, with more action.

"The Disappearance of Mr. Davenheim"
—*The Sketch*, March 1923

Odd to have two disappearance cases back to back in the collection, though their publications in *The Sketch* were also back to back—that is, a month apart. Also published as "Mr. Davenby Disappears."

In this tale, a rich financier vanishes from his home. Japp bets Poirot that he can't solve this case by merely sitting and thinking. Poirot, of course, ends up richer.

"The Adventure of the Italian Nobleman"
—*The Sketch*, October 1923

A return to murder, and high time! An Italian count is found dead, surrounded by evidence that he'd hosted a dinner party for three. The main suspect has an unbreakable alibi. Another good mystery, brimming over with red herrings.

"The Case of the Missing Will"
—*The Sketch*, October 1923

A young women's uncle dies and, in his will, leaves her his house for one year. If she can't find a second, later will in that time, his fortune will go to charity instead of her. She hires Poirot to help and he accepts, calling it "a problem charming and ingenious." And it is.

"The Veiled Lady"
—*The Sketch*, October 1923

Poirot is daydreaming of trying the criminal side of life when a lady gives him the chance, asking him to deal with a black-mailer for her. This story has been compared to Conan Doyle's "A Scandal in Bohemia" and there are some similarities.

"The Lost Mine"
—*The Sketch*, November 1923

Here we have a story narrated by Hastings, as told to him by Poirot. He's an entertaining storyteller, yet Hastings is not an active character. This is a secondhand telling, and the confused plot tries a little too hard to be mysterious through setting and characters alone.

"The Chocolate Box"
—*The Sketch*, May 1923

Another story within a story, again narrated by Poirot, but this is very well done. He relates his one failure, a poisoning case which he undertook while still with the Belgium police. This is one of my favorites in the collection (and not just because of the chocolate!). Also published under "The Clue of the Chocolate Box" and "The Time Hercule Poirot Failed."

THE UNDER DOG AND OTHER STORIES (1951)

This collection included stories from the early 1920s not published in Poirot Investigates. Some read like also-rans, perhaps those that didn't make the cut for the earlier collection, giving the title a double meaning. Over the next few decades, many of these tales were reworked into novelettes and other stories. I list them below not in the order they appeared in the anthology, but as close to chronological order as I can determine.

"The Affair at the Victory Ball"
—*The Sketch*, March 1923

Six people attending a fancy-dress ball masquerade as the six figures of the old Italian *Commedia dell'Arte*. The woman dressed as Columbine leaves early and is later found to have died of a cocaine overdose. The man dressed as Harlequin is found stabbed just before the ball's unmasking.

This was Christie's first story to use a Harlequin theme, on which she later based the entire series of Mr. Harley Quin shorts. If the first paragraph is any indication, this may well have been the first Poirot short that she wrote.

"The King of Clubs"
—*The Sketch*, March 1923

Four people are playing bridge when a woman—a famous dancer visiting the estate next door—staggers in, claiming she's witnessed a murder. Originally titled "Beware the King of

Clubs."

At the end of the story, Poirot points out what he believes to be a coincidence. It may be, or perhaps supernatural forces were at work. The reader is left to wonder. However, the story contains a second coincidence that is never explained, and therefore, regrettably, weakens the plot.

"The Plymouth Express"
—*The Sketch*, April 1923

A woman is found dead beneath a seat in a railway carriage. Her father, a rich American steel magnate, employs Poirot to find her murderer. Hastings' narration here is much more subtle, and completely absent in the interesting opening scene, which we see through the eyes of a sailor.

"The Market Basing Mystery"
—*The Sketch*, October 1923

Poirot and Japp investigate a suspicious suicide. A later tale, "Murder in the Mews," has too many similarities to be a simple borrowing of this plot. See chapter 11 for a comparison and fuller discussion of both.

"The Cornish Mystery"
—*The Sketch*, November 1923

Poirot deals with a woman who believes she is being poisoned by her husband. For more discussion and a comparison to "Death on the Nile" (not the novel, but the short featuring Mr. Parker Pyne), see chapter 11.

"The Adventure of the Clapham Cook"
—*The Sketch*, November 1923

A woman hires Poirot to find her cook, who walked off the job without giving notice. At first he balks, saying he's not a domestic service agency, but as the facts are laid before him, he becomes intrigued. A wonderful little puzzle. This has also appeared under "The Mystery of the Clapham Cook."

"The Submarine Plans"
—*The Sketch*, November 1923

Plans for a new submarine are stolen. See chapter 11 for more discussion and a comparison to "The Incredible Theft."

"The Lemesurier Inheritance"
—*The Sketch*, December 1923

The Lemesurier family curse states that no firstborn son shall inherit from his father. Over the centuries, all the eldest sons have died before their sires. When Hugo Lemesurier is diagnosed with an incurable disease, his firstborn son begins to have a series of accidents: near drowning, a bad fall, food poisoning. The boy's mother asks Poirot to investigate.

"The Under Dog"
—*London Magazine*, October 1926

This, the title story, is nearly 70 pages long, more like a novelette. A typical domestic murder, the characters and plot perhaps epitomize Christie's Poirot tales like no other, yet the pace seems slow, and the energy we expect from Christie's storytelling is inconsistent and usually lacking. The story feels overworked and under-edited. This was written not long after her mother died and while she was going through her divorce.

THE BIG FOUR (1927)

The Big Four is based on short mysteries first published in *The Sketch* in 1924. Christie rewrote the twelve stories, connecting them with a plot about an organization of master criminals, spreading the finished work over eighteen chapters. The result, as I mentioned earlier, is that most of the tales now read more like chapters in a novel than separate stories. However, since many other sources treat The Big Four as a short story collection, saying little about it at all, and since a few of the stories are worth reading even in their altered state, I've included the book here.

The tales were all first published within the first three months of 1924. Hastings' Watson-style of narration is back in evidence, though he's much less stiff than a year earlier. These stories also contain more action than the earliest Poirot stories.

Many of the chapter titles were changed from the titles of the stories as they first appeared in *The Sketch*. I've listed them below by original story title.

"The Unexpected Guest"
—*The Sketch*, January 1924

Captain Hastings returns to England from Argentina for a visit, only to find Poirot about to embark on a voyage to South America. Nothing can stop him, he claims, "unless," as Hastings quotes, "at the eleventh hour 'the door opens and the unexpected guest comes in.'" And that's precisely what happens.

"The Adventure of the Dartmoor Bungalow"
—*The Sketch*, January 1924

In the book, this story begins in the middle of chapter three ("We Hear More About Li Chang Yen"), and continues through chapter four ("The Importance of a Leg of Mutton"). Character-wise, this tale is linked to the other stories, but the plot stands on its own fairly well, relating a rather grisly murder in Dartmoor.

"The Lady on the Stairs"
—*The Sketch*, January 1924

In the book, this is titled "The Woman on the Stairs." The case involves kidnapping, and the woman turns out to be Poirot's old love interest, the Countess Vera Rossakoff (see the story "Double Clue" below, which was published first). While the premise is interesting, the tale did not convert well to the novel plot and is rather disappointing.

"The Radium Thieves"
—*The Sketch*, January 1924

Unfortunately, this story was completely absorbed into the novel plot and can't stand on its own at all. It's a chapter in the book, no more.

"In the House of the Enemy"
—*The Sketch*, January 1924

On the surface this too is more like a chapter than a story, yet there are enough twists to redeem the ending. The fun of it comes from watching Hastings go undercover.

"The Yellow Jasmine Mystery"
—*The Sketch*, February 1924

This covers two chapters in the book: "The Yellow Jasmine Mystery" and "We Investigate at Croftlands." A man apparently dies by accident after falling head first into a gas fire, but first he dips his finger into his inkwell and scrawls the words "yellow jasmine" across his newspaper. This is an excellent mystery.

"A Chess Problem"
—*The Sketch*, February 1924

The two premiere chess masters of the world meet for a match, but after only a few moves, one falls over dead. Intriguing and ingenious.

This is probably the best story of this bunch, and the only one to be reprinted after <u>The Big Four</u> was published. For those readers interested in tracking it down elsewhere, try Ellery Queen's <u>101 Years' Entertainment</u> of the 1940s, *Ellery Queen's Mystery Magazine* in 1972, and Richard Peyton's <u>Sinister Gambits</u>, 1991.

"The Baited Trap"
—*The Sketch*, February 1924

An adventure/suspense story in which Captain Hastings must choose between saving his wife or Poirot. In the book, it takes up two chapters: "The Baited Trap" and "The Mouse Walks In."

"The Adventure of the Peroxide Blond"
—*The Sketch*, February 1924

Titled simply "The Peroxide Blond" in the book, Christie exhibits what would become her lifelong fascination with actors. In this tale, Poirot and Hastings try to track down a criminal who had left the acting profession within the last three years. In the book, again, this one reads more like a chapter.

"The Terrible Catastrophe"
—*The Sketch*, March 1924

All three remaining stories are definitely more in Christie's adventure/suspense mode than typical of Poirot stories, yet are very reminiscent of Holmes' Professor Moriarty tales. Still, don't look for much clever detection in this story. What makes it worth reading is Poirot's famous quote:

> "You surprise me, Hastings. Do you not know that all celebrated detectives have brothers who would be even more celebrated than they are were it not for constitutional indolence?"

And so we're introduced to Poirot's twin, Achille.

"The Dying Chinaman"
—*The Sketch*, March 1924

This is a continuation of the last story, and a set up for the next, and consists mainly of people pointing out to Hastings the fact that he's not terribly bright.

"The Crag in the Dolomites"
—*The Sketch*, March 1924

In the book, this is two chapters: "Number 4 Wins a Trick" and "In the Felsenlabyrynth." The action of the climax is like an Indiana Jones movie—complete with secret passages through mountains—as Poirot and Hastings have their final showdown with The Big Four.

THREE BLIND MICE AND OTHER STORIES (1950)

This collection (also called <u>The Mousetrap and Other Stories</u>) was a multiple-sleuth American collection published in 1950. Two of its three Poirot tales first saw print in the 1920s, the other in 1940.

"The Adventure of Johnnie Waverly"
—*The Sketch*, October 1923

This story was first published as "The Kidnapping of Johnnie Waverly." The patriarch from one of England's oldest and wealthiest families is warned that his son will be kidnapped on a specific day and time. He takes precautions, but the boy disappears seemingly out from under the noses of his father and the police. Captain Hastings returns as narrator.

"The Third Floor Flat"
—*Detective Story Magazine*, January 1929

A woman, on bringing three friends back to her fourth floor apartment after a night out, realizes she doesn't have her key. Using an unorthodox method to gain entry to her flat, they accidently discover a dead body in the apartment below. Poirot, fortunately, has rented the flat on the fifth floor. One unique element of this story was recycled from "The Adventure of the Cheap Flat" in Poirot Investigates.

"Four and Twenty Blackbirds"
—*Colliers*, November 1940

A man always comes to a certain restaurant on Tuesdays and Thursdays, and for long enough that the waitresses learn his gastronomic preferences. One week, he shows up on a Monday and orders three foods he never liked before. A few weeks later, on his usual Thursday, he orders the same sort of unusual meal, and dies later that night. Also published under "Poirot and the Regular Customer."

As for the title, Christie also uses lines of this particular nursery rhyme for titles of two other works: "Sing A Song of Sixpence" (1934), and the novel A Pocket Full of Rye (1953), which plot-wise, was based on the second verse of the rhyme.

THE ADVENTURE OF THE CHRISTMAS PUDDING (1960)

This was a British anthology published in 1960. Four of its five Poirot stories were printed in earlier collections.

"The Adventure of the Christmas Pudding"
—original version: *The Sketch*, December 1923

As the source above implies, Christie wrote two versions of this tale. The first was also run under the title "Christmas Adventure." Sometime between the original publication in *The Sketch* in 1923 and this anthology in 1960, Christie reworked the tale, updating and expanding it, possibly for another periodical.

I recently came across a foreword and dedication Christie wrote for this story. No source or date was given, but since she wished her readers a happy Christmas, I believe the introduction was printed either with the first periodical publication, or with a reprint of that version, or with a periodical publication of the rewrite. In it, Christie described the tale as "an indulgence of my own, since it recalls to me, very pleasurably, the Christmases of my youth." She dedicated it "to the memory of Abney Hall—its kindness and its hospitality." Abney Hall was the home of her sister and brother-in-law. Anyone wanting to read the dedication should check their libraries for a copy of Thomas Godfrey's anthology <u>Murder for Christmas</u> (1962).

In the later version, Christie reset the story in the 1950s and expanded it into a novelette, which has also appeared under the title "The Theft of the Royal Ruby" (see <u>Double Sin and Other Stories</u>).

The last thing Poirot wants is an invitation to spend "an old-fashioned Christmas in the English countryside" in a drafty fourteenth-century manor house. He prefers the nice toasty radiators of his apartment. Only when assured that Kings Lacey has oil-fired central heating does he waver, and only because the holiday includes an interesting case involving a jewel robbery. In solving the case, Poirot finds that an old-fashioned Christmas isn't so bad after all, especially under the mistletoe.

This story, like many that Christie lengthened into novelettes, doesn't seem to fit its new, larger size. The pacing is slow—there were times I wanted to tell the characters to shut up and get on with the plot. Yet, it's worth reading if only for Poirot's reaction to staunchly British Yuletide customs, and for the last few lines, inspired, no doubt, by Dickens's "A Christmas Carol."

DOUBLE SIN AND OTHER STORIES (1961)

Three of the four Poirot shorts in this anthology were first published in the late 1920s. These stories show clear development in Christie's writing style. They are thoroughly engaging tales, with the energy that would define her detective stories henceforth.

"The Double Clue"
—The Sketch, December 1923

Countess Vera Rossakoff, Poirot's version of Holmes's Irene Adler, makes her debut here. She appeared again in <u>The Big Four</u> (1927). The plot centers on two clues that are left at the scene of a robbery. Also titled "The Dubious Clue."

"Wasp's Nest"
—The Daily Mail, November 1928

"Wasp's Nest" differs in that it was one of the first Poirot short stories *without* Hastings. It's also the first Poirot tale not written in first person. The point-of-view is third person, yet we're shown the action through Poirot's eyes and are only aware of his thoughts. This isn't a strong story, I think because, until now, the play between Hastings and Poirot has been so good as to sustain momentum. Poirot seems a little unsure how to act alone. Also titled "The Worst of All."

"Double Sin"
—Detective Story Magazine, March 1929

Poirot has business in Charlock Bay, but rather than riding the trains, Hastings talks him into a motor excursion (that is, a bus trip), which Poirot hates. En route, a young woman takes them into her confidence, and Poirot finds himself with an unexpected case. This story has also been titled "By Road or Rail."

"The Theft of the Royal Ruby"
—unknown, 1960

This story has been printed in various anthologies under the title "The Adventure of the Christmas Pudding," yet the original story of that name, first published in *The Sketch* in December 1923, is shorter and set right after World War I, with Poirot bemoaning the fact that his friend Hastings has moved to South America. See <u>The Adventure of the Christmas Pudding</u> above for a discussion of this longer version.

WITNESS FOR THE PROSECUTION (1948)

Only one Poirot story appeared in this collection:

"The Second Gong"
—*Ladies Home Journal*, June 1932

This locked room murder was later expanded into a novelette titled "Dead Man's Mirror." See chapter 11 for a full discussion and comparison of these two stories.

THE REGATTA MYSTERY (1939)

This includes several Poirot tales from the 1930s.

"The Mystery of the Bagdad Chest"
—*Royal Magazine*, January 1932

Couples dance while a murder takes place in the same room. No one sees or hears anything. See chapter 11 for a full discussion of this story and comparison to "The Mystery of the Spanish Chest."

"How Does Your Garden Grow?"
—*Ladies Home Journal*, June 1935

Miss Lemon, after making her debut as Parker Pyne's secretary in 1934 (see chapter 8), switches employers and now works for Hercule Poirot. She isn't quite his sidekick, but does play straight man, bringing out the charming imp in Poirot, a trait seldom seen since Hastings departed. In the story, an old woman writes Poirot a letter that says next to nothing, yet intrigues him, especially when the lady dies suddenly five days later. Two years after this story was published, the novel Poirot Loses a Client appeared, with a similar plot. Two more years and Easy to Kill (a.k.a. Murder is Easy) came out, with another elderly woman who, right before her death, tells the protagonist (not Poirot this time) that she's on her way to Scotland Yard about a murder, yet says very little else that makes sense.

"Problem at Sea"
—*Royal Magazine*, December 1935

This story has also appeared under the title "Poirot and the Crime in Cabin 66" and was a forerunner to the novel Death on the Nile. As in the novel, Poirot is on a cruise to Egypt (bemoaning, as always, his *mal de mer*). A new bride is murdered in her cabin. The husband was ashore in the company of other passengers at the time. Unlike the novel, the reader is told a few of the essential clues too late for a sporting chance at solving this one. The storytelling, however, is excellent. A slight error on Christie's part: Poirot claims in the story that he's never been to Egypt. See "The Adventure of the Egyptian Tomb" above.

"Yellow Iris"
—*Royal Magazine*, July 1937

A half hour before midnight, Poirot receives a mysterious phone call, summoning him to a nightclub and the "table with yellow irises." He finds a table set for six, but only five persons arrive, none of whom admit to the phone call. The sixth place is in memory of Iris Russell, who died at the club exactly four years before, murdered by one of those present. The conclusion isn't as satisfying as most of Christie's stories, but doesn't detract from the read.

She gets it right in <u>Remembered Death</u> (also titled <u>Sparkling Cyanide</u>) a novel expanded from "Yellow Iris" and published in 1945. The two works are similar only in plot and in the names of a few characters (including Iris, who is not the victim this time). Christie tells the stories very differently and, interestingly, leaves Poirot out of the novel.

"The Dream"
—*The Saturday Evening Post*, October 1937

A man tells Poirot of a recurring dream he has where he commits suicide by shooting himself at a specific time in the afternoon. Later, the man apparently does shoot himself, in the same manner and at the same time as in his dream. Poirot, however, remembers one of the victim's questions: Could a person somehow be murdered this way? An intriguing puzzle.

MURDER IN THE MEWS / DEAD MAN'S MIRROR (1937)

Four Poirot novelettes, or longer shorts, appeared in this anthology, and all of these tales are sans Hastings. Three of these novelettes were longer versions of earlier stories, and another was later lengthened into a novel.

"Triangle at Rhodes"
—*Royal Magazine*, May 1936

This is usually listed as a novelette, but really, the length is only slightly longer than average for a Christie short. In it, Poirot encounters murder and a love triangle on the Greek island of Rhodes. Delightfully presented. See chapter 11 for a full discussion and comparison to "Problem at Pollensa Bay," "The Blood-Stained Pavement," and the novel Evil Under the Sun.

"Murder in the Mews"
—original to this collection, 1937

This is Christie's second story published in 1937 to use murder disguised as suicide. In this one, a woman returns to her house in London to find her housemate dead. See chapter 11 for a full discussion of this novelette and a comparison to an earlier Poirot short, "The Market Basing Mystery."

"Dead Man's Mirror"
—original to this collection, 1937

Written in twelve short chapters, this is about a third the length of one of Christie's regular novels. Mr. Satterthwaite from the Mr. Quin series makes a cameo appearance in the first chapter. See chapter 11 for a full discussion and comparison of this story with "The Second Gong."

"The Incredible Theft"
—original to this collection, 1937

As in a normal short story, this was written in sections rather than chapters, but the overall feel is more like a novel.

The setting and characters—guests at a country manor—are too similar to "Dead Man's Mirror" to appear in the same book (possibly why this tale was originally left out of the American version). In both, Poirot is serious and candid—not his usual self.

The story is a retelling of "The Submarine Plans," only this time, the stolen plans are for a bomber. See chapter 11 for further discussion and a comparison of both stories.

THE LABORS OF HERCULES (1947)

Though this collection appeared in the late 1940s, at least three of the stories were written as much as seven years earlier. Christie had played with collections of linked stories before, first in 1927 when she strung twelve Poirot stories together in THE BIG FOUR, changing them enough to take away their ability to stand alone as short stories. That experiment was only semi-successful and was closer in final form to a novel than a collection. In 1929, Partners in Crime was published, a wonderful linked collection featuring Tommy and Tuppence Beresford (discussed in chapter 5).

Now Christie returns to the linked anthology with The Labors of Hercules. In the introductory chapter, titled "How It All Came About," we find Poirot once again pining after retirement and free time to cultivate vegetable marrows (a type of zucchini). He decides, after reading the exploits of his namesake, to accept only twelve more cases, chosen "with special reference to the twelve labors of ancient Hercules."

Her writing style is mature in these works, and the stories are confident and consistent. Poirot is now fully three-dimensional. The storytelling is excellent, delightfully impish and tongue-in-cheek. I found only one tale disappointing—the rest are among her best works. The titles are taken from the original Greek myths.

"The Nemean Lion"
—original to this collection, 1947

For this case, Poirot expected—promised himself—a "Lion" of great importance. Royalty perhaps, he muses, with a commendation at the Palace afterward. In the end, though, he takes on a case of Pekinese dognapping, chosen for its apparent *unimportance*. You might find it under the boring alternate title "The Case of the Kidnapped Pekinese."

"The Lernean Hydra"
—original to this collection, 1947

Poirot finds himself up against the many-headed hydra of village gossip when he investigates the death of a doctor's wife. As he gets to the bottom of each rumor, two more seem to appear. But like Hercules, he eventually finds the root and with it, the murderer. This was also published under the title "The Invisible Enemy."

"The Arcadian Deer"
—original to this collection, 1947

Poirot's expensive car breaks down on a snowbound country lane. While his chauffeur sees to repairs at the village garage,

Poirot spends the time at an inn called The Black Swan. The garage mechanic, who looks like "a young shepherd in Arcady," asks the detective to locate a young lady who's disappeared. This story has the feel of a fairy tale. Also titled "The Vanishing Lady."

"The Erymanthian Boar"
—original to this collection, 1947

In Switzerland, ten thousand feet above sea level, Poirot stalks a master criminal—a renown killer—and the members of his gang. Also published as "Murder Mountain."

"The Augean Stables"
—original to this collection, 1947

The mess and smell Poirot is expected to clean up is the rumor of scandal "in the highest political circles." Like Hercules, the little detective uses a force of nature strong enough to turn the course of the rumor. A glimpse of Christie's humor is evident in this one and it's my personal favorite in the collection.

"The Stymphalean Birds"
—original to this collection, 1947

At a resort in Herzoslovakia, two women use blackmail to prey on guests. This was also published under the titles "Birds of Ill-Omen" and "The Vulture Women." This story seems very straightforward on the surface, with the two women being the obvious villains. The plot, however, isn't straightforward at all, but I can't say more without giving it away.

"The Cretan Bull"
—original to this collection, 1947

A young man is convinced he's inherited his family's genes for homicidal insanity and breaks off his engagement. His fiancée doesn't give in so easily and consults Poirot. The detective, always a sucker for young lovers, agrees to help out. Later published as "Midnight Madness."

"The Horses of Diomedes"
—*Royal Magazine*, June 1940

In the original Greek legend, these horses ate human flesh. Poirot's flesh-eaters push cocaine. A wonderful story with modern-day overtones. This was one of only two Labors to be published in a periodical prior to the anthology, and has also appeared under the unimaginative title "The Case of the Drug Peddler."

"The Girdle of Hyppolita"
—*Royal Magazine*, July 1940

After saying he'd only take these twelve cases, the reader might wonder why Poirot would accept a job that obviously doesn't interest him—an unimaginative art theft. On top of that, as a favor to Inspector Japp, Poirot takes on a second case, the disappearance of a child named Winnie King. All is explained, of course, at the end. This also appeared under the title "The Disappearance of Winnie King." Part of this story is reminiscent of "The Kidnapped Prime Minister" in <u>Poirot Investigates</u>.

"The Flock of Geryon"
—original to this collection, 1947

The "flock" are members of a religious cult that preys on wealthy, lonely women. A little obvious, I thought, but a good read. Also titled "Weird Monster."

"The Apples of Hesperides"
—original to this collection, 1947

Another art theft, that of a golden goblet that once belonged to Roderigo Borgia. This is the one story in the collection that left me with questions. Christie may have been trying too hard to incorporate aspects of the Greek story to the detriment of the mystery. Also published as "The Poison Cup."

"The Capture of Cerberus"
—original to this collection, 1947

Vera Rossakoff, Poirot's one and only fatal fascination, returns again, and now owns a nightclub that's being used by the drug trade. Cerberus is the name of her large canine bouncer. The tale has also appeared under the appropriate title, "Meet Me in Hell." This story is fun—a perfect ending to the collection, and a fitting conclusion for the long run of Christie's Poirot shorts.

Chapter 5
The Couple Dressed in Parody

In her autobiography, Christie said, "<u>Partners in Crime</u> featured in it my two young sleuths, Tommy and Tuppence, who had been the principal characters in my second book, <u>The Secret Adversary</u>. It was fun to get back to them for a change."

"Fun" is what Christie had in mind when she wrote the stories for this collection, published in 1929. Tommy and Tuppence Beresford, now married and finding "happily ever after" a bit dull, eagerly accept an assignment from Mr. Carter of the Secret Service. They go undercover as the new owner and confidential secretary of a detective agency suspected of having connections with a spy ring. While waiting for the spies to show up, though, they must solve other cases as well.

Knowing nothing of the private eye business, Tommy and Tuppence decide to employ the methods of their favorite fictional sleuths. Hence, each story is a parody of and a tribute to different detectives created by writers who Christie admired. The methods are nicely varied, from Father Brown's atmospheric mysteries to the procedurals of Edgar Wallace. Others include the alibi-breaking Inspector French and, of course, Sherlock Holmes.

Of her choices, Christie later said, "It is interesting in a way to see who of the twelve detective-story writers that I chose are still well known—some are household names, others have more or less perished into oblivion. They all seemed to me at the time to write well and entertainingly in their different fashions."

This collection should be read in order, for the stories are all linked by the ongoing spy plot. Christie's sense of humor runs rampant in this work, not only in the way Tommy and Tuppence try to imitate their fictional colleagues, but in the way these two interact with each other and with their butler-turned-office boy, Albert. Albert does some playacting of his own, adopting the mannerisms of cinema stock characters.

The Beresfords are, I admit, my favorite Christie sleuths. They're an even match, neither playing Watson to the other's Holmes for very long. Tommy and Tuppence give off an energy not found in Christie's other series characters, a combination of youth and uninhibited personalities. Mr. Carter describes them as having "excessive self-confidence." They can be outlandish, donning priest's garb or assuming a French accent, just to get a feel for their roles, but they're also intelligent and caring, so as a reader, I feel sympathetic and want them to succeed.

Regrettably, they appear in only four novels and this one short story collection. It's a recurring dream of mine that in my lifetime, in an attic somewhere, will be found a large trunk filled with unpublished Tommy and Tuppence short stories of the caliber of this collection.

PARTNERS IN CRIME (1929)

"A Fairy in the Flat"

This isn't a story, but a short introductory chapter, explaining how Tommy and Tuppence assume the roles of Mr. Theodore Blunt and Miss Robinson of the International Detective Agency. Albert initially plays the part of a "Long Island butler."

"A Pot of Tea"
—*The Sketch*, September 1924

Albert happily trades his butler role for "office boy" complete with "paper bag of sweets, inky hands, and a tousled head." But a week after Tommy and Tuppence begin operations, they're still waiting for clients who want something besides having their spouses followed. Tuppence, ostensibly bored, goes off to buy a new hat. That trip to the hat shop brings in their first customer: wealthy Lawrence St. Vincent. He's got a missing person case, the solving of which gets Blunt's Brilliant Detectives publicity in the highest places. This also appeared as "Publicity."

"The Affair of The Pink Pearl"
—*The Sketch*, October 1924

Tommy, deciding that they are amateurs at investigations, brings his mystery novels to the agency to read up on techniques. When a friend of the St. Vincents asks Mr. Blunt to find a lost, possibly stolen, valuable pink pearl, Tommy decides to try the methods of Dr. John Thorndyke, written by R. Austin Freeman. Tuppence points out that there's nothing medico-legal about the case, but Tommy is dying to use his new camera, so off they go to photograph the crime scene. And in a way, it's the camera that allows them to find the pearl.

"The Adventure of The Sinister Stranger"
—*The Sketch*, October 1924

Having been told by Mr. Carter to keep watch for a letter in a blue envelope with a Russian stamp, the Beresfords are thrilled when such a letter arrives, but while they're reading it, a sinister stranger shows up. He consults them, yet they don't know if he's genuine, or if the gang of spies is trying to lead them into a trap. This, they decide, is a case for Okewood of the Secret Service—that is, Desmond Okewood and his brother Francis, created by Valentine Williams.

"Finessing The King" and "The Gentleman Dressed in Newspaper"
—*The Sketch*, October 1924

These are two chapters of the same story. Tuppence claims that, as detectives, they could use some practice. She sees an intriguing personal ad in the paper, which she interprets as saying something would happen at a little underground club at midnight after the Three Arts Ball. She suggests to Tommy that they should go and see if she's right.

". . . what you want," her husband says, "is to go to the Three Arts Ball and dance!" Tuppence convinces him in the end and they attend the ball dressed as American ex-cop Tommy McCarty and his best friend Dennis Riordan (by Isabel Ostrander). Afterward, in the club, the Beresfords overhear a murder, then solve it.

"The Case of The Missing Lady"
—*The Sketch*, October 1924

"If you must be Sherlock Holmes," Tuppence says to her husband, "I'll get you a nice little syringe and a bottle labeled Cocaine, but for God's sake, leave that violin alone." This after an impromptu recital by Tommy almost scared off their client. He's a famous Arctic explorer who's returned from an expedition only to find his fiancée missing. This tale, originally titled "The Disappearance of Mrs. Leigh Gordon," is one of my favorites.

"Blindman's Buff"
—*The Sketch*, November 1924

With business slack, Tommy decides to explore the world of Clinton H. Stagg's "Blind Problemist" Thornley Colton. Tommy dons opaque glasses, takes up a white cane, and has Tuppence be his "eyes" by telling him how many paces to the door. Experiments inside the office are half successful and he resolves to wear his "eyeshade" when they go to lunch, so he can test his developing senses. At the restaurant, a new and dangerous case presents itself. Despite his "blindness," Tommy must save himself and Tuppence.

"The Man in the Mist"
—*The Sketch*, December 1924

A typical G. K. Chesterton Father Brown mystery (yes, Tommy dresses as a Catholic priest), complete with atmosphere and a sense of fate. A famous but not terribly bright actress asks the Beresfords to stop at a certain house on their way to the train station. The route takes them down a little-used lane that runs by a cemetery, and they walk it through a thick fog. At the house, they find a recent murder and too few suspects.

"The Crackler"
—*The Sketch*, November 1924

No sooner do Tommy and Tuppence lament their lack of cases involving gangs, which would enable them to employ Edgar Wallace's methods, when Scotland Yard asks them to help crack a counterfeiting ring. The case allows Tuppence to flirt shamelessly with a younger man, while Tommy keeps company with a femme fatale. Originally titled "The Affair of the Forged Notes."

"The Sunningdale Mystery"
—*The Sketch*, October 1924

Tommy wants to try the methods written by Baroness Orczy, though almost relents when Tuppence insists that, if he's pretending to be the Old Man In The Corner, he must eat milk and cheesecake, foods he loathes. She encourages him by playing Polly Burton and eating cold tongue. Together they solve a case of murder on a golf course. First titled "The Sunninghall Mystery."

"The House of Lurking Death"
—*The Sketch*, October 1924

Next, a beautiful girl hires Mr. Blunt to find out who delivered a box of arsenic-laced chocolates that made everyone ill. Tommy thinks A. E. W. Mason's Inspector Hanaud is the right sleuth for the job, but he and Tuppence arrive at the house only to find that all the key players have been poisoned.

"The Unbreakable Alibi"
—*Holly Leaves Magazine*, December, 1928

This was the last Tommy and Tuppence short to be published in a periodical, and may have been written years after the others, not long before <u>Partners in Crime</u> came out.

To help a love-smitten, though not terribly bright young man, the Beresfords agree to solve a puzzle involving an unbreakable alibi. Since Freeman Wills Crofts' Inspector French always excels at breaking alibis, he's their model. The only problem with this story is that the main clue seemed too obvious.

"The Clergyman's Daughter" and "The Red House"
—Grand Magazine, December 1923

Originally titled "The First Wish," this was the first Tommy and Tuppence story to see print in a periodical.

The two titles above reflect two chapters in the collection. Instead of Tommy taking the part of the sleuth and Tuppence his sidekick, their roles are reversed as Tuppence dons the hat of Anthony Berkeley's Roger Sheringham. The plot is discussed in chapter 11, with a comparison to Miss Marple's "Strange Jest."

"The Ambassador's Boots"
—The Sketch, November 1924

Since Tuppence loves gobs of hot butter on her muffins, and since she can repeat "My dear fellow!" rather convincingly, she decides to become H. C. Bailey's Dr. Fortune, with Tommy playing Superintendent Bell. The case involves what appears to be an accidental switch of suitcases. But if not an accident, who would want the ambassador's boots?

"The Man Who Was No. 16"
—The Sketch, December 1924

The collection is topped off with an excellent parody of Christie's own work, as Tommy attempts to use the little gray cells of Hercule Poirot. This tale is a take-off on <u>The Big Four</u> (see chapter 4), hence the emphasis on the number sixteen (four squared). The plot is also the culmination of the ongoing book story, where Tommy and Tuppence at last tackle the spy ring, with near tragic circumstances.

In the final lines, we find an explanation of why this has to be their last case. I think Christie meant to keep it that way, but then World War II gave her the opportunity to play with spies once more. She couldn't resist taking the Beresfords out of mothballs, as a middle-aged couple, for the novel titled N or M?.

Chapter 6
A Man of Magic

Mr. Harley Quin is Christie's most unusual protagonist. He was, in her words, "a catalyst, no, more—his mere presence affected human beings . . . a friend of lovers, and connected with death." In the stories, Mr. Quin says of himself that he "comes and goes," usually suddenly, and no one knows to or from where.

He's based on a stock character of the *Commedia Dell'Arte*—that is, the Italian comedies of the sixteenth through eighteenth centuries in which Harlequin always helped young couples surmount obstacles to their happiness. When Christie was seventeen or eighteen, she wrote a set of poems on the Harlequin legend. Mr. Quin is a carry-over from that, and these stories were Christie's favorites.

She refused to write serial stories about Mr. Quin for periodicals, saying, "I only wanted to do one when I felt like it." This may have been sentimentality, or more likely, she simply had to be in the right frame of mind to write these unique tales. Possibly for the same reason, Mr. Quin never appeared in a novel.

THE MYSTERIOUS MR. QUIN (1930)

The twelve stories in The Mysterious Mr. Quin were written over a number of years, which explains the development in Mr. Quin's character from amateur detective to the true mysterious catalyst Christie wanted him to be.

The supporting character, Mr. Satterthwaite, also develops. He describes himself as "the most insignificant of men" and as a "listener and looker-on." Yet when Harley Quin is near, Mr. Satterthwaite becomes an actor in the drama. Mr. Satterthwaite believes events are, at times, manipulated by Mr. Quin himself. Like Harley Quin, Mr. Satterthwaite was a favorite character of Christie's. She used him again in the novel Murder in Three Acts (1935) and in the novelette "Dead Man's Mirror" (1937— see a discussion of this story in chapter 4). In both works, he and Poirot's personalities compliment each other beautifully.

But back to Mr. Quin. He's a supernatural character, not human, though only Mr. Satterthwaite sees him for what he is, aided by convenient stained glass lighting effects which turn Mr. Quin's clothes to the motley of Harlequin. Yet, with all this other-worldly symbolism, only one of the stories falls into Christie's Twilight Zone genre: the last one, "Harlequin's Lane."

Two of the others are more romance than mystery: "Soul of the Croupier" and "Man From The Sea." The rest are bona-fide mystery puzzles, extremely well done, the recurring themes being suicides that aren't suicides, ghosts that aren't ghosts, and people never being what they seem. The lesson learned by Mr. Satterthwaite is that events are better understood when seen from the distance of time.

Choosing favorites from this collection is difficult. They're all well-written. Still, I'd have to list "The Coming of Mr. Quin," "The Sign in the Sky," "The Face of Helen" and "The Dead Harlequin" as my preferences.

As for order, "The Coming of Mr. Quin" should definitely be read first. Reading the first seven stories in order is a good way to see the development of character. The next four can be read in any order, but I'd save "Harlequin's Lane" for last. The tale is eerie and unsettling, just the right note to end the Mr. Quin experience.

I also recommend not reading the whole collection in one sitting, or even within the space of a week. The stories are more intense than Christie's other works, and deal with unhappy, often morose, people. As with Christie's writing of them, reading these stories requires the right mood. Read them only when you feel like it.

Two other Mr. Quin stories were published in subsequent collections: "Love Detectives" and "The Harlequin Tea Set."

"The Coming of Mr. Quin"
—*Grand Magazine*, March 1924

This reads like the final scene of a whodunit. The story has gone before, and now, as the facts are reviewed, everyone suddenly realizes the truth. Mr. Quin is in the role of detective, yet the facts are brought to light by the others present. Mr. Satterthwaite plays his small part in the revealing, but is mostly an observer. Originally titled "The Passing of Mr. Quin."

"The Shadow on the Glass"
—*Grand Magazine*, October 1924

A mystery based around a ghost legend—a stain that forms on a certain window that, from a distance, resembles a Cavalier looking out (picture one of those seventeenth century fellows with long hair, frilly shirt and sword). Again, Mr. Quin is the detective, showing up at the crucial moment, but Mr. Satterthwaite plays a larger part.

"At the Bells and Motley"
—*Grand Magazine*, November 1925

Mr. Satterthwaite runs into Mr. Quin unexpectedly at an inn called the Bells and Motley. Together they review the three month-old disappearance of a country gentleman from the area. Mr. Satterthwaite does the solving this time, but with considerable prompting from Mr. Quin. Originally titled "A Man of Magic."

"The Sign in the Sky"
—*Grand Magazine*, July 1925

A nice little alibi puzzle, with Mr. Satterthwaite doing all the legwork this time and Mr. Quin mentoring. My only complaint is that Mr. S. shows a slowness akin to Hastings and Mr. Quin has to practically spell out the solution.

"The Soul of the Croupier"
—*Flynn's Weekly*, November 1926

As mentioned above, this story is not a mystery, but more of a romance. Frankly, I didn't think it had enough meat on it to be satisfying, but the ending is cute.

"The World's End"
—*Flynn's Weekly*, November 1926

Mr. Quin once again plays puppeteer, assembling in an out-of-the-way place those who had been involved in a year-old jewel theft, and just in time to save a life. This story is like watching a master magician perform an illusion.

"The Voice in the Dark"
—*Flynn's Weekly*, December 1926

Mr. Satterthwaite comes into his own as a sleuth, with a little encouragement from his mystic friend, in this second ghost mystery. Parts of the "howdunit" aren't satisfactorily explained, but the solution is clever.

"The Face of Helen"
—original to this collection, 1930

An excellent story, taking Mr. Satterthwaite and Mr. Quin to the opera. The method of murder is imaginative, though probably a bit farfetched, given the technology of the times. I can't say more without spoiling the ending.

"The Dead Harlequin"
—original to this collection, 1930

A supposed suicide which becomes a locked-room murder, after Mr. Satterthwaite sees it through an artist's eye. Still another ghost, and more supernatural overtones, but only (like Mr. Quin himself) as a story catalyst.

"The Bird with the Broken Wing"
—original to this collection, 1930

A Ouija board spells out Q-U-I-N, then the name of the place that Mr. Satterthwaite had been invited to dinner and overnight. He quickly calls his hostess to say he's changed his mind and will come. Sure enough, there's a murder, which Mr. Satterthwaite this time solves alone, without consulting his friend.

"The Man From the Sea"
—original to this collection, 1930

This is another romance. Mr. Satterthwaite vacations on a Mediterranean island, where he meets a depressed young man and a recluse in a rundown villa. After being told of a stranger seen nearby, in fancy harlequin dress, Mr. S. knows he's been called upon to once more act in a drama, rather than sit on the sidelines as usual.

"Harlequin's Lane"
—*The Storyteller*, May 1927

This is story deals more with the Harlequin legend than any of the others, and Christie creates a wonderful mood of supernatural creepiness as a backdrop. The ending is disturbing, yet absolutely right.

THREE BLIND MICE AND OTHER STORIES (1950)

"Love Detectives"
—*Flynn's Weekly*, October 1926

This story fits between stories #3 and #4 above, though it was actually first published between #4 and #5, under the title "At the Crossroads." For some reason, it was left out of the original Mysterious Mr. Quin collection.

Mr. Satterthwaite and a local magistrate are on their way to the scene of a murder when they encounter Mr. Quin. Mr. S. and his friend work as a duo in this tale, reconstructing the crime and once more saving the happiness of a young couple.

THE HARLEQUIN TEA SET (1989)

"The Harlequin Tea Set"
—Winter Crimes 3, 1971

Christie wrote this story for the Winter Crimes 3 anthology when she was 81 years old. It's her last published story and very likely the last one she wrote. Mr. Satterthwaite is the protagonist this time, with a mere cameo appearance by Mr. Quin. The narrative is third person, but, like first person, we are shown only Mr. Satterthwaite's thoughts and feelings.

This is the most realistic and poignant characterization of an acutely elderly person I've come across in all fiction. Mr. Satterthwaite is now forgetful and appears often confused. Even when the reader is shown that he's not as befuddled as he seems, Mr. Satterthwaite doesn't express his conclusions well.

Neither does Christie express herself well by this time and the story, as a mystery, is lacking, in need of clearer explanation at the end and less reminiscence and meandering at the beginning. I wonder how much of Mr. Satterthwaite's condition is crafted and how much is Christie's own elderly mind. Still, the characterization makes the story worth the read.

Chapter 7
Miss Marple Tells a Story

Miss Jane Marple, the elderly spinster whose observations of village life in St. Mary Mead allowed her to solve murders, was Christie's second most popular sleuth.

Yet, even though she was such a popular character, Christie published a mere twenty Miss Marple short stories in all, thirteen in one original Miss Marple anthology. The remaining seven tales showed up in three other collections, mixed in with Poirot, Pyne, and other stories. An anthology called 13 Clues for Miss Marple appeared in 1966, but all those stories had appeared in earlier anthologies.

THIRTEEN PROBLEMS / THE TUESDAY CLUB MURDERS (1932)

Miss Marple's debut came in December of 1927, when *Royal Magazine* published "The Tuesday Night Club" to begin a series of six short stories. The premise was simple: Six members of a dinner party agree to meet each Tuesday night. Each person would take a turn at telling of an unsolved mystery, which the others would then try to solve. The Tuesday Night Club, as they call themselves, consists of:

Raymond West, a writer
Joyce Lemprière, an artist
Sir Henry Clithering, former Commissioner of
    Scotland Yard
Dr. Pender, elderly clergyman of the local parish
Mr. Petherick, a solicitor
Miss Jane Marple, Raymond's aunt

"A representative gathering" Joyce observes, though she doesn't at first count Raymond's Aunt Jane. Miss Marple is easy to overlook as she knits quietly in her chair by the hearth, becoming more a part of the scenery in her old house. But she's included at last, if only because Joyce insists they need six people to play. Aunt Jane not only plays, but draws parallels in each case to some village incident before revealing the murderers.

In this *Royal Magazine* 1927-28 experiment, Christie found Miss Marple an interesting enough character to quickly put her into six additional stories, then a novel: <u>Murder at the Vicarage</u> (1930). The shorts were later combined, one last story added to make thirteen, and the collection published as <u>Thirteen Problems</u>, or <u>The Tuesday Club Murders</u>, in 1932 (possibly this latter title was chosen because <u>Thirteen Problems</u> was too easily confused with the Poirot novel <u>13 For Dinner</u>, published the same year).

All of the stories in this collection are well-written and highly recommended. I present them below as they appeared in the collection, since they flow best this way.

"The Tuesday Night Club"
—*Royal Magazine*, December 1927

The Tuesday Club is formed and Sir Henry, since he's the one law officer present, is asked to tell the first story. "The facts are

very simple," Sir Henry says. "Three people sat down to supper
. . . all three were taken ill . . . the third died." He goes on to
state the details of the case and gives everyone a chance to
guess the solution. Only Miss Marple is able to do so, after
relating the scandalous doings of Mr. Hargraves who lived on
the Mount. A delightful debut.

"The Idol House of Astarte"
—Royal Magazine, 1928

The clergyman, Dr. Pender, tells of once seeing a man struck
down, apparently stabbed, though no weapon was found and
no person was near the victim at the time. A wonderful howdunit, with a hint of the supernatural.

"Ingots of Gold"
—Royal Magazine, 1928

This is a story of pirates and buried treasure, yet Raymond
West is a stuffy, formal narrator, reminiscent of Hastings at his
most Watsonesque. This style makes the first part of the tale
seems to drag. Yet when all the other characters join in with
their guesses, the pace is redeemed.

"The Blood-Stained Pavement"
—Royal Magazine, 1928

Joyce Lemprière's story encompasses a theme that Christie
used several times over, involving murder at a seaside resort.
See chapter 11 for a full discussion and comparison with
"Triangle at Rhodes," "Problem at Pollensa Bay," and <u>Evil
Under the Sun</u>.

"Motive v. Opportunity"
—*Royal Magazine*, 1928

Mr. Petherick tells of a client of his who wrote a will in the lawyer's presence. Mr. Petherick slid the will into an envelope, brought it back to his office, and placed it into his safe. When the client died and the envelope was opened, it contained a blank sheet of paper. The two people who had the opportunity to tamper with the envelope benefitted most from the will, thus had no motive. The two who had a motive to tamper with it had no opportunity. This tale is somewhat reminiscent of Poirot's "The Case of The Missing Will."

"The Thumb Mark of St. Peter"
—*Royal Magazine*, 1928

The last of the actual "Tuesday Club" stories is told by Miss Marple herself. When the husband of her niece, Mabel Denman, dies suddenly, people begin saying Mabel poisoned him. Miss Marple finds out what, and who, killed Mr. Denman.

"The Blue Geranium"
—*The Storyteller*, December 1929

Though this and the next six stories first appeared in a variety of publications, it's obvious that Christie wrote them fairly close together, since, like the Tuesday Club, they all have the same setting and characters.

A year after the Tuesday Club, Sir Henry Clithering returns to St. Mary Mead to visit his friends, the Bantrys. When he suggests that Miss Marple should be invited to a dinner party, his host is taken aback ("Quite a dear, but hopelessly behind the times"). In the end, the host agrees, and so another gathering of six begins.

"The Blue Geranium" is the first mystery of the evening and involves a fortuneteller's fatal prediction and wallpaper flowers that change colors. Together they make for an intriguing tale.

"The Companion"
—probably first published in this anthology, 1932

At the same dinner, Dr. Lloyd tells of an incident that happened while he had a practice in the Canary Islands. One day, two old-maid tourists arrive on the island. The next day, one of them drowns while bathing, as the other tries to rescue her. All witnesses maintain it was an accident, except one, who says that the one woman deliberately held the other's head underwater.

This may have been printed in a periodical first, but I could find no publication earlier than this anthology.

"The Four Suspects"
—*The Pictorial Review*, January 1930

When Sir Henry's turn comes to tell a story, he tells of a man who helped break up a dangerous underground organization, dealing in "blackmail and terrorisation," that formed after World War I. The man then became a target of the members of the group who were still at large. He settled in England and eventually died of a apparent accident, but Sir Henry isn't convinced. Yet, only four suspects had the opportunity.

"A Christmas Tragedy"
—*The Storyteller*, January 1930

This was first published as "Never Two Without Three: A

Christmas Tragedy." Miss Marple tells of a Christmas holiday she once spent at a spa. A married couple arrived, and Miss Marple claims she could tell, just by looking at the husband, that he was bent on murdering his wife. The wife was subsequently killed in what appeared to be a robbery attempt. The husband had a foolproof alibi at the time.

"The Herb of Death"
—unknown, 1928

Mrs. Bantry remembers a dinner she and her husband attended where foxglove leaves had been mistakenly picked along with sage and used in duck stuffing. Everyone got sick and "one poor girl—Sir Ambrose's ward—died of it." Mrs. Bantry is a refreshing storyteller, simply because she refuses to go into detail, forcing her guests to think of questions. Miss Marple, as usual, draws the village parallel and solves the case.

This story seems to have been printed in a periodical in 1928, but sources are vague or differ as to exactly which publication.

"The Affair at the Bungalow"
—probably first published in this anthology, 1932

The last of the stories from Mrs. Bantry's dinner party is told by Jane Helier, a drop-dead gorgeous actress with very little functioning grey matter. Her tale involves a struggling playwright who's lured to a bungalow, drugged, and left as the scapegoat after the bungalow is burgled.

Again, I could find no earlier publication for this story.

"Death by Drowning"
—first published in this anthology, 1932

The only story not to take place at a dinner party, this one was likely written specifically for the collection, to make thirteen.

On a future stay with the Bantrys, Sir Henry is asked by Miss Marple to look into a local drowning case. Everyone thinks it was suicide, but Miss Marple is certain the girl was murdered and goes so far as to write down the name of the killer on a slip of paper. Sir Henry, paper in pocket, goes off to investigate. Miss Marple, of course, proves correct.

THE REGATTA MYSTERY (1939)

"Miss Marple Tells A Story"
—original to this collection, 1939

This story was written only a few years after The Tuesday Club Murders, but before the next Miss Marple novel was published. The narrative style is very different. Miss Marple tells this tale in first person, conversationally, while sitting with her nephew Raymond and the artist from the first anthology. This woman is now apparently Raymond's wife, or at least his girlfriend. Oddly enough, her name has changed from Joyce to Joan. No setting is given for this conversation, but I picture them as they were in many previous stories, around a hearth after dinner.

Mr. Petherick also makes a reappearance, in the story itself. Miss Marple tells of a problem he relates to her: an innocent man accused of stabbing his wife. On the evidence, only the husband or the chambermaid could have done it and the maid had no motive. Miss Marple, of course, shows who the murderer is in the end.

The story is simple, but the intimacy of the style carries it beautifully. I confess, in a few places I wanted to strangle Miss Marple for dithering too much, yet the story has a great deal of energy because of it.

THREE BLIND MICE AND OTHER STORIES (1950)

"The Tape-Measure Murder"
—*Royal Magazine*, February 1942

The original title of this story was "The Case of the Retired Jeweller."

When Mr. Spenlow's wife is murdered, everyone in St. Mary Mead thinks he did it. Miss Marple doesn't think so. Mr. Spenlow had been coming to her for gardening advice and she feels she knows him. Besides, after talking to Constable Palk, Miss Marple sees quite clearly who the killer is.

"The Case of the Perfect Maid"
—*Royal Magazine*, April 1942

The Skinner sisters fire their local maid. They bring in a new maid from a London agency who seems too perfect in every way. Miss Marple tells the Skinners to watch their silver. A theft follows, but with a twist.

"Strange Jest"
—original to this anthology, 1950

A young engaged couple seeks out Miss Marple for help. Their uncle always assured them they'd inherit his money when he died, yet, when he does pass away, no money or assets can be found. This tale is discussed in full in chapter 11, along with a comparison to Tommy and Tuppence's "The Clergyman's Daughter/The Red House." I could find no earlier publications for this tale and the next. They were likely written for this collection.

"The Case of the Caretaker"
—original to this anthology, 1950

Christie returns to her recurring theme of recovering from the flu. Miss Marple is the germ's victim this time, and to cheer her up, her doctor presents her with a mystery about a tragic accident involving a young, newlywed woman and a horse. This tale is a precursor to the novel Endless Night (1967).

DOUBLE SIN AND OTHER STORIES (1961)

"Sanctuary"
—*Women's Journal*, October 1954

Bunch Harmon, the wife of the vicar of Clipping Cleghorn, made her debut in A Murder is Announced (1950). She's also Miss Marple's godchild and a perfect sidekick for the elderly sleuth. Miss Marple can sit and detect, but Bunch is young enough to do the legwork and get into all sorts of trouble. Here is Bunch again, four years later, finding a dying man in her husband's church. The stranger says "sanctuary" before he dies, leading Bunch to wonder where he was from and why he came to Clipping Cleghorn to get shot.

This is a fast read, though the scenes in it sometimes seem to change rather abruptly, as if Christie had grown too accustomed to the slower pace in writing novels. Also, this is another story where the clues are presented a bit too late for the reader to feel included in the solution. Still, the team of Miss Marple and Bunch make the read worthwhile.

"Greenshaw's Folly"
—*Woman's Journal*, August 1960

One house in Raymond West's neighborhood is called Greenshaw's Folly, due to its extravagant size and lack of any one architectural style. The Greenshaw that still lives there is the elderly granddaughter of the builder and herself a notorious recluse. Raymond's niece by marriage, Louise Oxley, is hired by Greenshaw's granddaughter to compile the old man's diaries for publication. Louise is there a mere two days when she witnesses a murder.

This story is filled with Christie's trademark components: the eccentric elder making a will, the austere housekeeper (described by one of Raymond's friends as the type to put arsenic in the teapot), the gardener who does very little gardening, and several other elements unmentionable without giving away the plot.

I've come across one source that states this story may have been published in a periodical as early as 1957, but most sources give the 1960 date.

Chapter 8

The Case of the Retired Statistician

Mr. Parker Pyne is another of Christie's series characters to appear solely in short stories, and is perhaps the most unlikely of her protagonists.

Formerly, as a government statistician, Mr. Pyne spent years compiling facts and figures about the general population. He's a quintessential clerk, a quiet man who doesn't draw attention to himself. Yet, he's intensely interested in people, if only to be able to classify them, much the way an entomologist sorts bugs.

Upon his retirement, he decides to use this knowledge to solve people's problems, specifically, to make them happy. He opens an agency, placing an ad in the papers: "Are you happy? If not, consult Mr. Parker Pyne . . ." Most of the time, he's not a sleuth at all. His primary role is usually not as investigator, but as instigator.

All Parker Pyne stories originated in the 1930s. Christie never returned to him later, as she did most of her other sleuths, perhaps because he wasn't really detective material.

PARKER PYNE INVESTIGATES / MR. PARKER PYNE: DETECTIVE (1934)

Of the twelve tales in this collection, six can't be called true detective stories, so both the English and American titles are only half accurate. Yet these first six stories are delightful, creative and unorthodox, containing enough mysterious doings to satisfy the staunchest addict.

In the last six tales, Mr. Pyne does solve crimes, though compared to Christie's other sleuths, he seems a somewhat lackluster detective. His charm rests in his eagerness to interfere and make things happen, not simply sit back and wait for the truth to bring enlightenment àla Poirot. Still, the stories are well-written, with classic Christie twists. "The Oracle at Delphi" stands out among them.

The book is also notable in that both Miss Lemon and Mrs. Ariadne Oliver make their first appearances here. Before going to work for Poirot, Miss Lemon is Mr. Pyne's secretary, and the famous mystery writer Ariadne Oliver (Agatha Christie's parody of herself) apparently picks up a little money on the side helping Mr. Pyne re-write reality (impossible to say more without spoiling the tales). Mrs. Oliver makes her novel debut just a few years later in the Poirot mystery, <u>Cards on the Table</u>.

The stories in this collection can be read out of order, but they have a certain "variations on a theme" quality which is best appreciated in the sequence they're presented. Just when you catch yourself thinking, "Oh, she did this in the *last* story," Christie throws in yet another curve.

I couldn't find earlier periodical publications for many of these stories. The tales that did appear in periodicals were all published as stand-alones, not as series.

"The Case of the Middle-Aged Wife"
—first published in this collection, 1934

A woman's husband has a mid-life crisis that doesn't include her. Mr. Pyne arranges for her to have a mid-life crisis of her own. This is our first glimpse of Miss Lemon, described as "a forbidding-looking young woman with spectacles."

"The Case of the Discontented Soldier"
—*Cosmopolitan*, 1932

A retired soldier finds life back in England dull, until Mr. Pyne has Mrs. Oliver rewrite the soldier's life for him. Mrs. Oliver is already a "sensational novelist," author of "forty-six successful works of fiction, best-sellers in England and America, and freely translated into French, German, Italian, Hungarian, Finnish, Japanese, and Abyssinian." And, of course, her trademark bag of apples sits beside her typewriter.

"The Case of the Distressed Lady"
—first published in this collection, 1934

Since there's a crime involved, this one's closer to a true detective story than any other of the first six, though we already know "who done it." A woman tells Mr. Pyne that she has stolen an acquaintance's diamond necklace, but feels remorse and wants to return it. The trick is, she wants to return it before anyone finds out. Mr. Pyne takes the matter into his own hands. The twist at the end is exquisite. One of my favorite Pyne stories.

"The Case of the Discontented Husband"
—first published in this collection, 1934

This is a variation on "Middle-Aged Lady," with the wife having the mid-life crisis and her hubby upset about it. The ending is completely different, though.

"The Case of the City Clerk"
—first published in this collection, 1934

A mild-mannered clerk, who lives an unexciting life but reads suspense books, expresses a wish for adventure. He wants to get out of his rut just once in his life. Mr. Pyne arranges some spy work for him. Things get out of hand. A fun read.

"The Case of the Rich Woman"
—first published in this collection, 1934

This is my favorite Parker Pyne story. A woman from modest roots has come into money over the course of her lifetime, but she's lost happiness. Mr. Pyne returns her interest in life to her, in a very unorthodox way.

"Have You Got Everything You Want?"
—*Cosmopolitan*, April 1933

Here begins Mr. Pyne's detective stories, this one first published under the title "Express to Stamboul."

Just after Christie's divorce, she decided to travel by herself. "I should find out what kind of person I was," she said in her autobiography, "—whether I had become entirely dependant on other people as I feared." Her destination was Baghdad, and her transportation was the Orient Express to

Stamboul. Out of this trip came her famous novel <u>Murder on the Orient Express</u>, but also this short story.

In this tale, Mr. Pyne is taking that train when an American woman finds out who he is and consults him en route about some words she noticed on her husband's ink blotter.

My only gripe is that, like many other of Christie's American characters, the lady speaks with an English accent, using phrases like "you've not been very successful." Christie's idea of American speech involved the placement of the word "just," as in "I've been just mean."

Yet, despite that, this is a fine mystery.

"The Gate of Baghdad"
—first published in this collection, 1934

In this tale, Christie recounts some of the events of her own first road trip across the desert, including the car becoming mired in the sand. Her traveling companion was Max Mallowan, who later told her he'd decided she'd make a good wife then and there because she didn't fuss when the car got stuck.

Christie puts Mr. Pyne on a six-wheeler bus with a handful of other passengers. Driving through the dark, they too become stuck, and the men disembark to try to free the vehicle. They realize one man is still on the bus. When they go to rouse him, they find him dead. Murdered. Mr. Pyne solves the case and, like Christie, manages to get out of the desert alive.

"The House at Shiraz"
—first published in this collection, 1934

Not long after marrying Max, Christie traveled to the Middle East with him again and this time they visited Shiraz. "We went to one beautiful house, I remember," she wrote. ". . . I used it as the setting for a short story . . ."

Parker Pyne finds a mad Englishwoman living in that house. She dresses in native clothes and absolutely refuses to admit visitors. Yet, when Mr. Pyne sends his card and a copy of his famous advertisement ("Are you happy? If not, consult Mr. Parker Pyne . . ."), she agrees to see him.

"The Pearl of Price"
—first published in this collection, 1934

This one is set at Petra—the place in Jordon with the amazing buildings carved into the sides of a canyon. You know, where Indiana Jones found the Holy Grail.

This is also the first story of Christie's to show an insider's view of archaeology. As a group of travelers tour the ruins, one of them has a valuable pearl that goes missing. See chapter 11 for a full discussion and comparison to "The Regatta Mystery."

"Death on the Nile"
—first published in this collection, 1934

The setting of this story is very much like its novel namesake (Death on the Nile, 1937): a cruise on the Nile. The plot is completely different, yet we have a murder here, too, of a family matriarch who makes life miserable for all who accompany her.

"The Oracle at Delphi"
—first published in this collection, 1934

Mr. Pyne travels to Greece, where he encounters a doting mother and her eighteen year-old son. The son is kidnapped and ransom demanded but, unable to lay her hands on much cash so far from home, the mother decides to give the kidnappers her diamond necklace instead. That's where Mr. Pyne steps in. Of all stories where Parker Pyne solves a crime, this is my favorite.

THE REGATTA MYSTERY (1939)

Mr. Parker Pyne returns in two shorts in this collection. Personally, I think it's a shame that she didn't write more like the first six tales above and "Problem at Pollensa Bay" below, where, instead of investigation, Mr. Pyne is content to simply interfere in people's lives.

"The Regatta Mystery"
—Strand Magazine, 1936

While this title story is a good mystery and worth reading, the detective in it could as easily have been Poirot or Miss Marple instead of Parker Pyne, and the outcome would have been the same. In fact, I've come across sources referencing this as "Poirot and the Regatta Mystery" so I presume Christie wrote an alternate version with her Belgium detective. See chapter 11 for a full discussion and comparison to "The Pearl of Price."

"Problem at Pollensa Bay"
—Strand Magazine, 1936

Parker Pyne is at his unique nosy-parking best, even though this story was rewritten under different titles and with different detectives three times. For a full discussion and comparison to "The Blood-Stained Pavement," "Triangle at Rhodes" and <u>Evil Under the Sun</u>, see chapter 11.

Chapter 9

The Mystery of the Missing Detective

As we've seen so far, most of Agatha Christie's mystery stories feature a series detective: Poirot, Miss Marple, the Beresfords, Mr. Quin, or Parker Pyne. Yet several of her mystery stories include none of these sleuths. Some of her best crime stories— "Witness for the Prosecution" and "Philomel Cottage" for example—use no real detective character at all. In most of these non-detective tales, the protagonist is personally involved as victim, villain, witness or suspect.

The Hound of Death and Other Stories was a British collection published in 1933. Five of its stories fall into this non-detective type of mystery. A year later, in 1934, The Listerdale Mystery stories were all from this subgenre.

About that same time, Christie married her second husband, Max Mallowan, and she began playing with plays— writing original dramas or dramatizing short stories and novels.

"I had no idea when the idea was first suggested," Christie said, "what terrible suffering you go through with plays . . ." But she must have liked them, because between 1934 and the end of her life, she wrote or co-wrote fifteen in all.

With that and writing novels, this would be reason enough for curtailing her short story output. Only three non-series-detective mysteries were published after 1934.

THE HARLEQUIN TEA SET (1989)

"The Actress"
—*Novel Magazine*, May 1923

This wonderful little story may be Christie's first use of an actor/actress character. The acting profession intrigued her greatly, and she would go on to create many more actor/actress characters in later novels. This story is about a crime, and so I call it a mystery, but it's more of a howdunit than a whodunit. Also titled "A Trap For The Unwary."

"The Mystery of the Spanish Shawl"
—*Novel Magazine*, August 1928

This story has been confused in other chronologies with "The Mystery of the Spanish Chest" and its partner "The Mystery of the Bagdad Chest." It has no relation to either. Actually first published under the title "The Mystery of the Second Cucumber," it then became "Mr. Eastwood's Adventure" (see The Listerdale Mystery collection below).

    The plot revolves around a mystery writer with a bad case of block. Inspiration comes, but at a price. One of Christie's lightest mysteries.

"Manx Gold"
—*Daily Dispatch*, May 1930

In 1930, Christie was commissioned to write a story containing clues for the *Isle of Man Treasure Hunt Scheme*, a promotion meant to increase tourism to the island. At the end of April that year, she visited the island, met the promoters, and together they decided where the "treasures" would be hidden and what the clues would be. The next month, the Manchester

Daily Dispatch printed the first of five installments, and published five other clues separately. Also, brochures on the island carried the story for all tourists. Readers who wanted to participate were advised to bring a map of the island, guide-books, and certain folklore and history books.

Unfortunately, readers today need to take the same mea-sures to follow the story. Because this was written as a real scavenger hunt, the narrative leaves out many details and clues found along the way. Still, it's easy to see how much fun she had coming up with the mystery and with the idea of sending people off in all the wrong directions.

The reprint in The Harlequin Tea Set contains a foreword, explaining the commission and planning, and an afterword, explaining the clues and revealing the solutions, who the win-ners were, how they managed it, and what they won.

THE HOUND OF DEATH AND OTHER STORIES (1933)

"The Red Signal"
—*Grand Magazine*, June 1924

This story has all the trappings of one of Christie's supernatural stories, with premonitions, talk of insanity, and even a séance. At heart, though, it's a solid murder mystery with a solution that in no way hinges on the occult. Another of my favorites.

"The Mystery of the Blue Jar"
—*Grand Magazine*, July 1924

Each day at 7:25 a.m., a man hears a woman cry "Murder! Help, murder!" as he plays his morning round of golf. Problem is, no one else hears it. The ghost of a murdered women? Or is this golfer in need of a shrink instead of a caddie?

"The Witness For The Prosecution"
—*Flynn's Weekly*, January 1925

This is one of Christie's most famous, beloved, and best short stories—an excellent study in twists. Every aspiring mystery writer ought to read and analyze it. Very simply, a man is accused of murder. The key to his alibi, his mistress, decides to testify against him.

I was a teenager when I first read this story. I've remembered the last line all my life, and it still gives me a chill.

Flynn's ran it under the title "Traitor's Hands," but the name was changed before inclusion in The Hound of Death (1933). In 1953, Christie dramatized the story. The play was very popular and was made into an excellent movie with Tyrone Power, Marlene Dietrich, and Charles Laughton in 1957. In 1982, a TV movie remake featured Diana Rigg.

The story can also be found in the Witness for the Prosecution anthology (1948).

"S. O. S."
—*Grand Magazine*, February 1926

After Mortimer Cleveland has two flat tires within ten minutes, he's forced to spend the night with a family in their lonely cottage out in the middle of Wiltshire Downs. He finds "S.O.S." written in the dust on his night table, and is certain one of the daughters did it, but which one?

"Wireless"
—*Mystery Magazine*, March 1926

"Wireless" was the title used both in its first publication and in

The Hound of Death collection, but American readers know this story better as "Where There's a Will," from the Witness for the Prosecution collection of 1948.

The plot is ingenious: a wireless radio is apparently used as a mode of communication for voices beyond the grave. The tale may appear transparent to the hardened Christie fan, but wait until the final twist before passing judgment.

THE LISTERDALE MYSTERY (1934)

"The Girl in the Train"
—*Grand Magazine*, February 1924

An adventure story evocative of Tommy and Tuppence, first published a mere two years after The Secret Adversary, and two months after the first Tommy and Tuppence short story hit the newsstand. The Beresfords are absent however.

The hero, newly fired from his uncle's firm, hops a train to go seek his fortune. Before he even leaves Waterloo Station, a pretty girl jumps into his carriage and begs him to hide her, which he does. So his adventure begins.

"Jane in Search of a Job"
—*Grand Magazine*, August 1924

Another early 1924 story with a Tuppence-like main character. The style of the story is also like Christie's "young adventurer" books.

Jane is out of work and practically down to her last penny when she answers a want ad that sounds rather like a casting call. She gets the job and an adventure to boot.

"Mr. Eastwood's Adventure"
—*Novel Magazine*, August 1924

Novel Magazine ran this story as "The Mystery of the Second Cucumber" before the title was changed for The Listerdale Mystery anthology. Under a third title, "The Mystery of the Spanish Shawl" (see above), the tale appeared in various other printings, including The Harlequin Tea Set.

As I noted in my description of that collection, this is one of Christie's lightest mysteries, about a mystery writer with a bad case of block.

"Philomel Cottage"
—*Grand Magazine*, November 1924

This is one of Christie's best stories and one of my favorites. I've read descriptions of it that claim the ending is open to interpretation, but I disagree—Christie clearly shows us the narrator's thoughts. Still, the last line makes one wonder. The tale is about the power of suggestion and is classic suspense, much like Hitchcock in style.

In 1936, Christie teamed up with Frank Vosper to dramatize the tale, a play titled *Love From a Stranger*.

"The Manhood of Edward Robinson"
—*Grand Magazine*, December, 1924

First titled "The Day of His Dreams," this tale tells of Edward Robinson, who finds that a new car can lead to mystery and romance, all in one day. See discussion and comparison to "A Fruitful Sunday" in chapter 11.

"The Listerdale Mystery"
—*Grand Magazine*, December 1925

Originally "The Benevolent Butler." In it, Mrs. St. Vincent mourns the loss of the family estate and her decline into genteel poverty, until she sees a similar house listed for a ridiculously low rent, with servants retained at the landlord's expense. She moves in with her son and daughter, but really, the situation seems too good to be true. And it is.

A few of Christie's stories from this time period have the recurring theme of a house or apartment on the market for very little cost. The tales aren't related otherwise, but rather, likely reflect Christie's own real estate experiences before settling into her Sunningdale home in 1924. She named the place Styles, after the house in her first novel.

"The Rajah's Emerald"
—*Red Magazine*, July 1926

Here we meet a man with the unfortunate name of James Bond. Christie used the name long before Ian Fleming, but anyone reading the story these days is bound to have the more popular persona come to mind, which makes the character of James Bond all the more ironic. He is a thoroughly unconfident young man who reads self-help books, yet he's so human in his self-doubts that he's lovable.

James wants his girlfriend to quit spending time with the more affluent and debonair Claude Sopworth. His decision to be more assertive lands him in a bigger mess, with a stolen emerald in his pocket and no good excuse for how it got there.

The mood and energy of this story bubble from the first sentence. Funny and delightful.

"Swan Song"
—*Grand Magazine*, September 1926

This is no whodunit, but a true suspense story. A prima donna soprano (along with, apparently, a good chunk of the opera company from Covent Garden), is commissioned to give a command performance of an opera at a country estate. She insists on doing *Tosca*. That decision sets in motion a chain of tragic events.

Being a musician myself, I'm often put off by the musician stereotypes I find in books, particularly the "prima donna" character, always temperamental and eccentric. Christie's singer is both of these, but the traits are shown as a costume the character assumes, as she would for any performance, to hide her real nature. She's a human and believable musician.

The story's only fifteen pages long, but reads like a longer work, possibly because it's broken into three segments, like the three acts of an opera.

"Accident"
—*The Daily Express*, 1929

Inspector Evans retires from the force and settles in a cottage in the country. There he recognizes a woman who'd been tried and acquitted of the murder of her husband nine years before. The jury had decided the death was more likely an accident than murder. The woman is now remarried and no one in the village knows of her past. Evans vows there will be no more "accidents" on his watch.

"Sing a Song of Sixpence"
—first published in this collection, 1934

An aging barrister comes to regret a decade-past shipboard

romance when the lady looks him up and asks him to investigate a murder. This story is so much in the mode of a Poirot tale, one wonders why Christie didn't use her famous detective in it. Possibly because Poirot would have been too ill with his *mal de mer* to engage in a romance. It's most noteworthy in that this may be her first use of a nursery rhyme element in a plot.

"A Fruitful Sunday"
—first published in this collection, 1934

This one is extraordinarily like "The Manhood of Edward Robinson" mentioned above: a car, romance, and even the same type of mystery. Yet they were published in the same anthology. See chapter 11 for a detailed discussion and comparison of both tales.

"The Golden Ball"
—first published in this collection, 1934

This story begins in much the same way as "The Girl in The Train" from the same collection: a man named George is fired by his uncle. After page one, however, this tale takes a completely different direction.

THREE BLIND MICE AND OTHER STORIES (1950)

"Three Blind Mice"
—first published in this collection, 1950

This is without doubt Christie's most famous story, not because it's been read more than the others, but because it's been seen more.

Not long after World War II ended, the BBC asked Christie if she could quickly write a short radio play for a program they were planning to honor the Queen Mother, who had specifically requested that something of Agatha Christie's be included. Christie wrote a twenty minute sketch entitled "Three Blind Mice."

Someone then suggested to her that she should expand the sketch into a short mystery, which she did. It became the title story in this 1950 collection.

However, Christie had been experimenting with writing stage plays. In 1951, *The Hollow* opened and proved a success, so Christie decided to further expand the story "Three Blind Mice" into a two-hour stage thriller. She added an extra character and a fuller background and plot. A play titled *Three Blind Mice* was already running, so she changed her title to *The Mousetrap*. It opened in 1952 and hasn't closed yet. Of its phenomenal success, Christie said,

> "I think one of the advantages *The Mousetrap* . . . has had over other plays is the fact that it was really written from a précis, so that it had to be the bare bones of the skeleton coated with flesh. It was all there in proportion from the first. That made for good construction."

On a personal note, I had the good fortune to work on props and set construction for a college production of *The Mousetrap*. This was one of the most fun plays I've ever been involved in and also, from the viewpoint of details and timing, one of the most difficult. Through full rehearsals and performances, as I watched from the back of the house (after having set things like suitcases and skis in their correct places), I never tired of watching it. I always got caught up in the story, and always feared for the life of the main character at the right moment. Listening to audience reaction night after night, I have to say it was one of the most satisfying plays I've had a hand in.

But back to the short story. In many sources, this is listed as a novelette. It's around 70 pages and Christie's average for a short story is closer to 20. Still, I call it a long short story because it reads that way, tight and fast.

If you've seen the play, you'll find Miss Casewell missing from the read, but the up side is that you get to enjoy Christie's prose. From the opening prologue through the descriptions of Monkswell Manor, Molly's thoughts, and each characterization, the reader can see exactly how Christie pictured the story in her own mind. "Three Blind Mice" ought to be required reading for all would-be directors and designers of future productions of *The Mousetrap*.

Chapter 10

The Call of Romance, the Supernatural, and Dogs

Christie's first stories were of the supernatural, and she continued to write in this genre even after her detective stories became popular.

Some are tales of horror and imagination in the Poe tradition. Some are games of what-if, amazing flights of imagination, offering unorthodox and often unnerving explanations for the unexplained. Many explore the subjects of immortality, insanity, power, premonitions, and what might be called the occult side of romance.

In my opinion, these tales are some of her finest stories, perhaps because her imagination was most free in writing them, unrestrained by the format of the whodunit, or even by the limits of reality as we know it.

She also wrote several shorts which are essentially love stories, though they tend to be unorthodox, with great twists. I call them romances, but using the broadest definition of the word.

Here's a mystery for you: Christie talks of writing a story in her early years, before World War I, and giving it the title "Vision." The tale, she claimed, was inspired by May Sinclair's "A Flaw in the Crystal." Christie described it as a psychic story and said it was rewritten and "published with some other stories of mine in a volume much later." Yet no story titled "Vision" appeared in the collections published during her lifetime.

The Sinclair story is a rather long tale about a woman with a psychic power to cure depression in others, at the great cost of her own soul. None of Christie's shorts closely resembles the plot, though mental illness was a common theme. If I had to chose candidates for "Vision," based on Sinclair's tale, my short list would be "The Last Séance," "Fourth Man," or "The Edge." If you want to try solving the mystery yourself, see if you can find a copy of Sinclair's Uncanny Stories (published by MacMillan, New York in 1923), then read Christie's supernatural shorts for comparison.

THE HARLEQUIN TEA SET (1989)

"While the Light Lasts"
—*Novel Magazine*, April 1923

A romantic tragedy with vague supernatural elements which tend to blur the telling of the story. The setting is Africa, fresh in Christie's mind after visiting there on a trip around the world with her first husband. She may have even written it en route or as soon as she got home. How she was going to earn her keep was on her mind, apparently, given the choices of her main character.

"Within a Wall"
—*Royal Magazine*, October 1925

Another romantic tragedy, yet less about love and more about people's motives for their actions. Like "While the Light Lasts," this deals with why people get married. Unlike most Christie stories, I found the ending unsatisfying. I have to wonder if this reflects the problems she was having in her own marriage. Leaving the ending sad and somewhat unresolved may have seemed exactly right to her at the time.

"The Edge"
—*Pearson's Magazine*, February 1927

This is an excellent study in the psychology of power. The insanity theme reappears once more, as does the marriage theme, not surprising as this was written the year Christie's mother died and her first husband, Archie Christie, divorced her.

THE HOUND OF DEATH AND OTHER STORIES (1933)

The tales included in this collection were either straight supernatural stories or mysteries with paranormal elements, so it's a primary source for Christie's supernatural yarns.

"Fourth Man"
—*Grand Magazine*, December 1925

A lawyer, doctor, and clergyman decide to pass the time on a railway journey discussing a tragic and fantastic case of multiple personality syndrome. The fourth man in the carriage tells what he knows of the case, offering a more horrific explanation. One of Christie's best speculations.

"The Hound of Death"
—first published in this collection, 1933

A World War I-era nun has memories of a past life in an ancient civilization (Atlantis perhaps?) that had found the secret of harnessing all of earth's natural powers of destruction. The story is very surreal and creepy.

One line from the tale is "The events which I am relating took place in 1921," implying that this was written sometime later in that decade or in the early 1930s. As far as I can tell, it was never published before becoming the title story in this collection.

"The Gipsy"
—first published in this collection, 1933

A man has a lifelong fear of gypsies because of a recurring dream. This is a tale of second-sight and, in the end, ill-timed lives.

"The Lamp"
—first published in this collection, 1933

A genuine ghost story about a family that moves into a haunted house. Exquisitely chilling. Don't read it at night.

This reads very much like "The Call of Wings" and other early tales, but even if Christie wrote it earlier, it was apparently not published until The Hound of Death.

"The Strange Case of Sir Arthur Carmichael"
—first published in this collection, 1933

The young man of the title is found wandering about his village one morning in "a semi-idiotic condition, incapable of recognizing his nearest and dearest." At the same time, the phantom of a large grey cat is seen and heard around his family's estate. While this story does contain a good mystery, the supernatural element is dominant.

"The Call of Wings"
—first published in this collection, 1933

The story of a rich man who decides to shed his possessions. According to her autobiography, this is one of Christie's first stories. See chapter 3 for the full discussion.

"The Last Séance"
—first published in this collection, 1933

Another of Christie's first stories, this time about a medium who agrees to do one last séance before retiring. See chapter 3 for the full discussion.

THE GOLDEN BALL AND OTHER STORIES (1971)

"Magnolia Blossom"
—*Royal Magazine*, March 1926

A romantic tragedy following Christie's usual handling of the topics of love and marriage, but in the end, more about human manipulation.

"Next to a Dog"
—*Grand Magazine*, 1929

A great little romance for dog lovers. Also, very much a story about people's priorities in life: what they usually are versus, perhaps, what they should be. This feels like one of Christie's earliest stories and it's delightful.

THE REGATTA MYSTERY (1939)

"In a Glass Darkly"
—first published in this collection, 1939

A dark, brooding story of a man who sees a premonition in a mirror just before heading off to World War I. The premonition comes true in a surprising way. In style, this seems to be one of Christie's earlier stories, probably written not long after World War I, though I could find no publication of it before The Regatta Mystery. This may be her first use of a mirror as a plot device, which she repeats in other stories and novels. A nice creepy tale, and one of my favorites.

DOUBLE SIN AND OTHER STORIES (1961)

"The Dressmaker's Doll"
—*Woman's Journal*, 1958

A large puppet doll apparently moves around a dressmaker's shop all by itself. After reading this story, if you have any dolls or stuffed animals in your house, you'll find yourself doing double takes to make sure their eyes aren't following you around the room. One of her most original stories and another of my personal favorites.

Chapter 11

The Purloined Plot

Christie often reused plots, plot concepts, and even whole chunks of previous stories over the years. This began not long after her mother's death. Christie had been so distraught, she couldn't write a word, yet her first husband, Archie, wanted a divorce, so she needed money badly. Archie's brother, Campbell, suggested that "the last twelve stories published in *The Sketch* should be run together, so that they would have the appearance of a book." (This became The Big Four, discussed in chapter 4.)

Several short stories were expanded into novels or plays over the years (for instance "Yellow Iris" became Remembered Death—see chapter 4). These I note in the chapters where their detective or genre is discussed.

Below, however, I've listed those short stories that share plot and other aspects in common. Reading these works in chronological order can be fascinating.

"The Manhood of Edward Robinson"
—*Grand Magazine*, December 1924
and
"A Fruitful Sunday"
—The Listerdale Mystery, 1934

Oddly enough, both of these stories appear in The Listerdale Mystery collection of 1934.

To find the root of both tales, we have to go back to the early 1920s, when *The Evening News* paid Christie five hundred pounds for the serialization rights to The Man in the Brown Suit. When her husband, Archie, asked how she was going to spend the windfall, she, very sensibly, said she ought to save it for a rainy day. He suggested she buy a car. A car! No one in her circle of friends had a car. Cars were for the rich.

Reminiscing in her autobiography, Christie said that first car was one of two things that excited her most in her entire life. (The second was dining with the Queen forty years later.)

Almost immediately after she bought that car, she wrote "The Manhood of Edward Robinson," recreating her first motor-love, down to the five hundred pounds that bought it. To make it interesting, she added a diamond necklace in a most unlikely place, and a drop-dead-beautiful woman. For Edward Robinson, who'd only read of such things in dime store romances, this was a dream come true. A wonderful mystery, lighthearted and funny.

A mere three stories later in the same anthology, "A Fruitful Sunday" tells of another chap named Edward who's also just purchased a car (this time a used one for only twenty pounds). His girl may not be quite as drop-dead-gorgeous, but another necklace (rubies this time) turns up where least expected. Like "Manhood," "Fruitful Sunday" is a lighthearted and funny mystery. The two stories have completely different endings.

"The Cornish Mystery"
—*The Sketch*, November, 1923
and
"Death on the Nile"
—Parker Pyne Investigates, 1934

"The Cornish Mystery" is a typical early Poirot story with

Hastings playing Watson. As stated in chapter 4, a woman comes to Poirot saying she suspects her husband is poisoning her. Other characters in the story are a niece, the niece's fiancée, and of course, the husband. Poirot sees all and tells all. "The Cornish Mystery" was later included in The Under Dog and Other Stories (1951).

In the early 1930s, Christie took the same plot and characters, renamed everyone, placed them in Egypt, and substituted J. Parker Pyne as the sleuth. She titled that story "Death on the Nile" (no relation to the novel) and it was published in Mr. Parker Pyne, Detective in 1934.

I prefer the second version because the details seem better thought out. Yet I can't see why she didn't simply rewrite it as another Poirot story. It's much more in his line than Mr. Pyne's, who makes a better busybody than detective. Presumably Christie needed an extra Pyne tale and this plot just happened to be available. Neither story shows Christie's best storytelling.

"The Market Basing Mystery"
—*The Sketch*, October, 1923
and
"Murder in the Mews"
—Murder in the Mews/Dead Man's Mirror, 1937

Besides *The Sketch*, "The Market Basing Mystery" appeared in The Under Dog and Other Stories (1951). In the story, Hastings, Poirot and Inspector Japp are enjoying a stay in the country when the master of the local estate is found shot dead, an apparent suicide, since the door to the room was locked and the gun was resting in his right hand. The wound, however, is on the left side of his head. Inspector Japp is asked to assist; Poirot and Hastings tag along, but of course, Poirot solves the case. A good story but the narration, like many of Christie's early Poirot tales, is compromised by a sameness and stiffness.

"Murder in the Mews" appeared in <u>Murder in the Mews</u> (<u>Dead Man's Mirror</u>) in 1937. It's very obviously a retelling of "Market Basing" only this time, two women share a small house in London. One returns from a stay in the country to find her friend dead, the same apparent suicide. Another difference is that "Murder in the Mews" is a novelette, written in ten chapters. Unlike some of Christie's other novelettes (discussed below), this length fits this story, making it a fast read. Instead of Hastings' formal first person narration, Christie writes in third person. Inspector Japp makes a great straight man to the Belgian's antics, and Poirot himself gives a sparkling performance.

The two versions are separated by a fourteen-year gap. The development in Christie's style is amazing and worth noting.

"The Submarine Plans"
—*The Sketch*, November 1923
and
"The Incredible Theft"
—<u>Murder in the Mews</u>/<u>Dead Man's Mirror</u>, 1937

Also from <u>The Under Dog</u> comes "The Submarine Plans," and this time Hastings narrative style is relaxed and engaging. Poirot is called to the country estate of Lord Alloway, Head of the Ministry of Defense, after plans for a new submarine are stolen. Among the suspects are an admiral, a lady from London society, her French maid, and Alloway's secretary. The length of the story is a mere 17 pages.

In "The Incredible Theft" (<u>Murder in the Mews</u>/<u>Dead Man's Mirror</u>, 1937), the plans are for a new bomber, the host is Lord Mayfield, the admiral becomes an Air Marshall, and the lady is now from America. We still have a maid and a secretary in the same pivotal roles. The plot is the same otherwise, the biggest change being the absence of Hastings. Poirot does a solo. The other major difference is that the tale is stretched over 49 pages.

Though Christie's writing style is much improved by the second version, the plot works better in the shorter length. The flow of the story is slowed considerably and Poirot's energy level suffers for it. Also, without Hastings, or any other foil, Poirot is too serious.

"The Submarine Plans" may not be Christie's best short story, but it's a sound, decent read, and the right length. "The Incredible Theft" didn't do it justice.

"The Clergyman's Daughter"/"The Red House"
—*Grand Magazine*, December 1923
and
"Strange Jest"
—Three Blind Mice, 1950

Both of these stories deal with an old man or woman who prefers alternatives to simply making a will.

The first story appeared in the 1929 collection, Partners in Crime, split into two chapters, hence with two chapter titles, but in *Grand Magazine* it was published as "The First Wish." In it, Tommy and Tuppence Beresford are semi-professional private detectives who take on a case in which a woman has inherited her great aunt's estate, which includes a large house but not enough money to maintain it. Oddly enough, from the moment she takes possession, she's besieged with both extravagant offers to buy and strange poltergeist experiences that keep scaring off her paying guests. Tommy and Tuppence investigate to find out who wants the house so badly, and the case turns into a sort of treasure hunt. The tale is delightful and the clues well-placed.

"Strange Jest" was published in Three Blind Mice (1950), though may have been written earlier. In another story of missing money, Miss Marple joins in the hunt this time, which proceeds along the same lines as in "The Red House." An entertaining read, but unfortunately, the solution to the puzzle revolves around a little known saying, so readers may feel cheated.

"The Second Gong"
—*Ladies Home Journal*, June 1932
and
"Dead Man's Mirror"
—Murder in the Mews/Dead Man's Mirror, 1937

"The Second Gong" is an ingenious locked room murder that takes place just before dinner at a country estate. The story includes one of Christie's favorite elements: a smashed mirror. Luckily, one of the late-arriving dinner guests is Hercule Poirot. This non-Hastings tale begins even without the sleuth. We're allowed a good gander at all the suspects before Poirot arrives—that is, we get to know them through their speech and actions. Despite his lack of sidekick, Poirot is his charming, flamboyant, energetic self. This is a fun read.

"The Second Gong" was reprinted in the Witness for the Prosecution collection (1948).

In the mid-1930s, Christie rewrote the story, expanding it to more than three times its length into the novelette "Dead Man's Mirror." Poirot is present from the beginning, but the reader is given an entire chapter of plodding, secondhand character descriptions before he actually arrives at the murder scene and we meet the suspects. Poirot has even less pizzazz here than in "The Incredible Theft."

Like that novelette, this rewrite has too much padding, especially since the original short was so good. The result is like taking a stylish size 6 dress and adding scrap material helter-skelter to create a size 20. The proportion and flow come out all wrong.

I highly recommend "The Second Gong" over "Dead

Man's Mirror." Or read them both and see what you think.

"The Blood-Stained Pavement"
—*Royal Magazine*, 1928
"Triangle at Rhodes"
—*Royal Magazine*, May 1936
"Problem at Pollensa Bay"
—*Strand Magazine*, 1936
and
Evil Under the Sun

"The Blood-Stained Pavement" was one of The Tuesday Club Murders (1932), in fact, it was number four of the first six Miss Marple stories published. "Triangle at Rhodes" is a Poirot story included in Murder in the Mews/Dead Man's Mirror (1937). "Problem at Pollensa Bay" featuring Parker Pyne, appeared in The Regatta Mystery in 1939. The Poirot novel Evil Under the Sun made its debut in 1941.

All four of these stories share a seaside location and a *femme-fatale* character who comes between a happy couple.

During the late 1920s and through the 1930s, Dame Agatha obviously had love triangles on her mind. Considering that her own love life was finally beginning to settle down (with her second marriage to Max Mallowan), her inspiration probably wasn't entirely personal. Sure, the memories of her own triangle and subsequent divorce were still with her, but time and Max had brewed them into story fodder. Moreover, she was traveling a good deal (as are all the narrators of the above tales). She possibly came across similar characters or even a triangle situation, potential or real. Whatever the case, these stories were the result.

In "The Blood-Stained Pavement," Joyce, the artist in the Tuesday Club (see chapter 7), tells of encountering murder in a Cornish fishing village where she'd gone to do sketches. The triangle's there, but the significance isn't clear until Miss Marple puts her finger on the important clues. This is one of Christie's shortest stories. I think a few more paragraphs could have been added to make the plot clearer, and I found myself questioning the bloodstains themselves (I can't explain further without spoiling the plot). Still, the story is a very enjoyable read.

"The Triangle at Rhodes" is essentially the same plot as above, with a few different turns, a clearer presentation, and Poirot getting sand in his shoes. The opening scene, where Poirot sits on the beach (in his white suit), conversing with two young, sunbathing women, is delightful. The novel Evil Under the Sun, though it has more characters and different names, isn't much more than an expanded rewrite of "The Triangle at Rhodes." Personally, I prefer the shorter version.

Most other references, if they discuss short stories at all, don't include "Problem at Pollensa Bay" in a comparison of the stories mentioned above. For one thing, this isn't a murder mystery, but a classic Parker Pyne problem. For another, the triangle in this story might be said to have a fourth side: an interfering mother who wants Mr. Pyne to "save her boy." This is one of my favorite Parker Pyne tales.

"A Pearl of Price"
—Parker Pyne Investigates/Mr. Parker Pyne: Detective, 1934
and
"The Regatta Mystery"
—Strand Magazine, 1936

Interestingly enough, both of these stories feature Parker Pyne as detective. Other characters in common are an American man traveling abroad with his daughter, and a closed group of people who will all be suspects in the theft of a valuable object. In the first story, it's a pearl; in the second, a diamond. The object goes missing and the surroundings are searched to no avail. When it's evident that one of the group must be responsible, each person is also searched, again with no results. Mr.

Pyne, of course, eventually finds the impossible hiding place and recovers the bauble.

"A Pearl of Price" was written first, and published in the 1934 collection Parker Pyne Investigates (a.k.a. Mr. Parker Pyne: Detective). "The Regatta Mystery" came only a few years later, in the 1939 collection of the same name. The stories have distinctly different solutions.

"The Mystery of the Bagdad Chest"
—*Royal Magazine*, January, 1932
and
"The Mystery of the Spanish Chest"
—The Adventure of the Christmas Pudding, 1960

Many Christie references list these as the same story. The plot is the same, and several of the characters. In both, Poirot is the detective who finds the same murderer in almost the same way. However, ninety percent of the prose is completely different.

"Bagdad" is in first person, narrated by Hastings. The puzzle is clever and the story well told. You can find it in The Regatta Mystery, an American collection published in 1939.

More than twenty years later, "Spanish" appeared in the 1960 British collection The Adventure of the Christmas Pudding. It's in third person this time, with Miss Lemon instead of Hastings, although she has no more than a cameo role at the beginning. Besides the prose, a few character names were changed. Most first names were revised, or added if the character had only been called by a surname in "Bagdad." The telling of the story is expanded, more witnesses interviewed, more red herrings introduced. Certain elements were updated —for instance, the "phonograph" in the first story became "two stereophonic record players" in the second.

These two stories are worth reading together, if possible, for glimpses into Christie's creative mind at a twenty-plus year interval.

Conclusion
Have You Got Everything You Want?

In the following pages, to help you find the stories, Appendix A lists the shorts in alphabetical order with alternates titles and up to three anthology sources. The anthologies are in chronological order according to first publication, that is, Source 1 was the first anthology to include the story, Source 2 the second, etc.

For those readers who want the challenge of reading the short stories in the order of their earliest publication, Appendix B lists the tales in chronological order, also with alternate titles and series sleuth.

Appendix C lists the collections above in the order they were first published, with dates, alternate titles and series sleuth where appropriate. These anthologies have been reissued in various editions since Christie's death. Many are currently in print. In addition, new collections which include Christie's shorts appear from time to time. Finding most of the tales shouldn't be difficult.

What more can I say? Start reading!

THE END

Appendix A

AGATHA CHRISTIE'S SHORT STORIES
—in Alphabetical Order with Anthology Sources and Alternate Titles

Title	Source 1	Source 2	Source 3	Alternate Title
Accident	Listerdale Mystery	Witness for the Prosecution	13 for Luck!	
Actress, The	Harlequin Tea Set			A Trap For the Unwary
Adventure of "The Western Star", The	Poirot Investigates			
Adventure of Johnny Waverly, The	Three Blind Mice	HP's Early Cases	Surprise! Surprise!	The Kidnapping of Johnny Waverly
Adventure of the Cheap Flat, The	Poirot Investigates			Poirot Indulges a Whim
Adventure of the Christmas Pudding, version 1	(no anthology)			Christmas Adventure
Adventure of the Clapham Cook, The	Under Dog	HP's Early Cases		The Mystery of the Clapham Cook
Adventure of the Dartmoor Bungalow, The	The Big Four			
Adventure of the Egyptian Tomb, The	Poirot Investigates			

Title	Source 1	Source 2	Source 3	Alternate Title
Adventure of the Italian Nobleman, The	Poirot Investigates			
Adventure of the Peroxide Blonde, The	The Big Four			
Adventure of The Sinister Stranger, The	Partners in Crime			
Affair at the Bungalow	Tuesday Club Murders			
Affair at the Victory Ball, The	Under Dog	HP's Early Cases		
Affair of The Pink Pearl, The	Partners in Crime			
Ambassador's Boots, The	Partners in Crime			
Apples of Hesperides	Labours of Hercules			The Poison Cup
Arcadian Deer	Labours of Hercules	Surprise! Surprise!		The Vanishing Lady
At the Bells and Motley	Mysterious Mr. Quin	Surprise! Surprise!		A Man of Magic
Augean Stables	Labours of Hercules			

Title	Source 1	Source 2	Source 3	Alternate Title
Baited Trap, The	The Big Four	The Big Four		
Bird with a Broken Wing	Mysterious Mr. Quin	13 for Luck!		
Blindman's Bluff	Partners in Crime			
Blood-Stained Pavement, The	Tuesday Club Murders	13 Clues for Miss Marple		
Blue Geranium	Tuesday Club Murders	13 for Luck!	13 Clues for Miss Marple	
Call of Wings, The	Hound of Death	Golden Ball		
Capture of Cerberus	Labours of Hercules			Meet Me In Hell
Case of the Caretaker	Three Blind Mice	13 Clues for Miss Marple		
Case of the City Clerk, The	Mr. Parker Pyne			
Case of the Discontented Husband, The	Mr. Parker Pyne			
Case of the Discontented Soldier, The	Mr. Parker Pyne			

Title	Source 1	Source 2	Source 3	Alternate Title
Case of the Distressed Lady, The	Mr. Parker Pyne	Surprise! Surprise!		
Case of the Middle-Aged Wife, The	Mr. Parker Pyne			
Case of the Missing Lady, The	Partners in Crime			The Disappearance of Mrs. Leigh Gordon
Case of the Missing Will, The	Poirot Investigates			
Case of the Perfect Maid	Three Blind Mice	13 Clues for Miss Marple	Surprise! Surprise!	
Case of the Rich Woman, The	Mr. Parker Pyne			
Chess Problem, A	The Big Four			
Chocolate Box, The	Poirot Investigates	HP's Early Cases		The Clue of the Chocolate Box; The Time Hercule Poirot Failed
Christmas Tragedy, A	Tuesday Club Murders			Never Two Without Three
Clergyman's Daughter, The, and the Red House	Partners in Crime			The First Wish
Coming of Mr. Quin, The	Mysterious Mr. Quin			The Passing of Mr. Quin

Title	Source 1	Source 2	Source 3	Alternate Title
Companion, The	Tuesday Club Murders	13 Clues for Miss Marple		
Cornish Mystery, The	Under Dog	HP's Early Cases	Surprise! Surprise!	
Crackler, The	Partners in Crime			The Affair of the Forged Notes
Crag in the Dolomites, The	The Big Four			
Cretan Bull	Labours of Hercules			Midnight Madness
Dead Harlequin, The	Mysterious Mr. Quin			
Dead Man's Mirror	Dead Man's Mirror	Murder in the Mews		
Death By Drowning	Tuesday Club Murders			
Death on the Nile	Mr. Parker Pyne			
Disappearance of Mr. Davenheim, The	Poirot Investigates			Mr. Davenby Disappears
Double Clue, The	Double Sin	HP's Early Cases	Surprise! Surprise!	The Dubious Clue

Title	Source 1	Source 2	Source 3	Alternate Title
Double Sin	Double Sin	HP's Early Cases		By Road or Rail
Dream, The	Regatta Mystery	Adventure of the Christmas Pudding		
Dressmaker's Doll, The	Double Sin			
Dying Chinaman, The	The Big Four			
Edge, The	Harlequin Tea Set			
Ermanthian Boar	Labours of Hercules			Murder Mountain
Face of Helen, The	Mysterious Mr. Quin	13 for Luck!		
Finessing the King and the Gentleman Dressed in Newspaper	Partners in Crime			
Flock of Geryon	Labours of Hercules			Weird Monster
Four and Twenty Blackbirds	Three Blind Mice	Adventure of the Christmas Pudding		Poirot and the Regular Customer
Four Suspects, The	Tuesday Club Murders	13 for Luck!	13 Clues for Miss Marple	

Title	Source 1	Source 2	Source 3	Alternate Title
Fourth Man, The	Hound of Death	Witness for the Prosecution		
Fruitful Sunday, A	Listerdale Mystery	Golden Ball		
Gate of Baghdad, The	Mr. Parker Pyne			
Gipsy, The	Hound of Death	Golden Ball		
Girdle of Hyppolita	Labours of Hercules	13 for Luck!		The Disappearance of Winnie King
Girl in the Train, The	Listerdale Mystery	Golden Ball		
Golden Ball, The	Listerdale Mystery	Golden Ball		
Greenshaw's Folly	Double Sin	Adventure of the Christmas Pudding	13 Clues for Miss Marple	
Harlequin Tea Set, The	Winter Crimes 3	Harlequin Tea Set		
Harlequin's Lane	Mysterious Mr. Quin			
Have You Got Everything You Want?	Mr. Parker Pyne			Express to Stamboul

Title	Source 1	Source 2	Source 3	Alternate Title
Herb of Death, The	Tuesday Club Murders	13 Clues for Miss Marple		
Horses of Diomedes	Labours of Hercules			The Case of the Drug Peddler
Hound of Death, The	Hound of Death	Golden Ball		
House at Shiraz, The	Mr. Parker Pyne			
House of Dreams, The	Harlequin Tea Set			House of Beauty
House of Lurking Death, The	Partners in Crime			
How Does Your Garden Grow?	Regatta Mystery	HP's Early Cases		
Idol House of Astarte	Tuesday Club Murders			
In A Glass Darkly	Regatta Mystery			
In the House of the Enemy	The Big Four			
Incredible Theft, The	Dead Man's Mirror	Murder in the Mews		

Title	Source 1	Source 2	Source 3	Alternate Title
Ingots of Gold	Tuesday Club Murders			
Jane in Search of a Job	Listerdale Mystery	Golden Ball		
Jewel Robbery at the Grand Metropolitan	Poirot Investigates			The Curious Disappearance of the Opalsen Pearls
Kidnapped Prime Minister, The	Poirot Investigates			
King of Clubs, The	Under Dog	HP's Early Cases		Beware the King of Clubs
Lady on the Stairs, The	The Big Four			The Woman on the Stairs
Lamp, The	Hound of Death	Golden Ball		
Last Seance, The	Hound of Death	Double Sin		
Lemeurier Inheritance, The	Under Dog			
Lernean Hydra	Labours of Hercules			The Invisible Enemy
Listerdale Mystery	Listerdale Mystery	Golden Ball		The Benevolent Butler

Title	Source 1	Source 2	Source 3	Alternate Title
Lonely God, The	Harlequin Tea Set			
Lost Mine, The	Poirot Investigates	HP's Early Cases		
Love Detectives	Three Blind Mice			At The Crossroads
Magnolia Blossom	Golden Ball			
Man From the Sea, The	Mysterious Mr. Quin			
Man in The Mist, The	Partners in Crime			
Man Who Was No. 16, The	Partners in Crime			
Manhood of Edward Robinson, The	Listerdale Mystery	Golden Ball		The Day of His Dreams
Manx Gold	Harlequin Tea Set			
Market Basing Mystery, The	Under Dog	HP's Early Cases	13 For Luck!	
Million Dollar Bond Robbery, The	Poirot Investigates			The Million Dollar Bank Robbery

Title	Source 1	Source 2	Source 3	Alternate Title
Motive vs. Opportunity	Tuesday Club Murders	13 Clues for Miss Marple		
Miss Marple Tells a Story	Regatta Mystery			
Mr. Eastwood's Adventure	Listerdale Mystery	Witness for the Prosecution		The Mystery of the Second Cucumber, The Mystery of the Spanish Shawl
Murder in the Mews	Dead Man's Mirror	Murder in the Mews		
Mystery of Hunter's Lodge, The	Poirot Investigates			
Mystery of the Bagdad Chest, The	Regatta Mystery	Surprise! Surprise!		
Mystery of the Blue Jar, The	Hound of Death	Witness for the Prosecution		
Mystery of the Spanish Chest	Adventure of the Christmas Pudding	Harlequin Tea Set		
Nemean Lion	Labours of Hercules	13 for Luck!		The Case of the Kidnapped Pekinese
Next to a Dog	Golden Ball			

Title	Source 1	Source 2	Source 3	Alternate Title
Oracle at Delphi, The	Mr. Parker Pyne			
Pearl of Price, The	Mr. Parker Pyne			
Philomel Cottage	Listerdale Mystery	Witness for the Prosecution		
Plymouth Express, The	Under Dog	HP's Early Cases	Surprise! Surprise!	The Mystery of the Plymouth Express
Pot of Tea, A	Partners in Crime			Publicity
Problem at Pollensa Bay	Regatta Mystery	13 for Luck!		
Problem at Sea	Regatta Mystery	HP's Early Cases		Poirot and the Crime in Cabin 66
Radium Thieves, The	The Big Four			
Rajah's Emerald	Listerdale Mystery	Golden Ball		
Red Signal, The	Hound of Death	Witness for the Prosecution		
Regatta Mystery	Regatta Mystery	13 for Luck!		
S.O.S.	Hound of Death	Witness for the Prosecution		

Title	Source 1	Source 2	Source 3	Alternate Title
Sanctuary	Double Sin	13 Clues for Miss Marple		
Second Gong, The	Witness for the Prosecution			
Shadow on the Glass, The	Mysterious Mr. Quin			
Sign in the Sky, The	Mysterious Mr. Quin			
Sing a Song of Sixpence	Listerdale Mystery	Witness for the Prosecution		
Soul of the Croupier, The	Mysterious Mr. Quin			
Strange Case of Sir Arthur Carmichael, The	Hound of Death	Golden Ball		
Strange Jest	Three Blind Mice	13 Clues for Miss Marple		
Stymphalean Birds	Labours of Hercules			Birds of Ill Omen; The Vulture Women
Submarine Plans, The	Under Dog	HP's Early Cases		
Sunningdale Mystery, The	Partners in Crime			The Sunninghall Mystery
Swan Song	Listerdale Mystery	Golden Ball		

Title	Source 1	Source 2	Source 3	Alternate Title
Tape-Measure Murder	Three Blind Mice	13 for Luck!	13 Clues for Miss Marple	The Case of the Retired Jeweller
Terrible Catastrophe, The	The Big Four			
Theft of the Royal Ruby, The	Adventure of the Christmas Pudding	Double Sin		Adventure of the Christmas Pudding, version 2
Third Floor Flat	Three Blind Mice	HP's Early Cases	Surprise! Surprise!	In the Third Floor Flat
Three Blind Mice	Three Blind Mice			The Mousetrap
Thumb Mark of Saint Peter	Tuesday Club Murders	13 Clues for Miss Marple		
Tragedy of Marsdon Manor, The	Poirot Investigates			
Triangle at Rhodes	Dead Man's Mirror	Murder in the Mews		
Tuesday Night Club, The	Tuesday Club Murders			
Unbreakable Alibi, The	Partners in Crime	13 for Luck!		
Under Dog, The	Under Dog	Adventure of the Christmas Pudding		

Title	Source 1	Source 2	Source 3	Alternate Title
Unexpected Guest, The	The Big Four			
Veiled Lady, The	Poirot Investigates	HP's Early Cases	13 for Luck!	
Voice in the Dark, The	Mysterious Mr. Quin			
Wasp's Nest	Double Sin	HP's Early Cases		The Worst of All
Where There's a Will	Hound of Death	Witness for the Prosecution	Surprise! Surprise!	Wireless
While the Light Lasts	Harlequin Tea Set			
Within a Wall	Harlequin Tea Set			
Witness for the Prosecution	Hound of Death	Witness for the Prosecution	Surprise! Surprise!	Traitor's Hands
World's End	Mysterious Mr. Quin			
Yellow Iris	Regatta Mystery			
Yellow Jasmine Mystery, The	The Big Four			

Appendix B

AGATHA CHRISTIE'S SHORT STORIES

—in Chronological Order with First Publication and Date.

Title	Earliest Date	Series Character	First Publication	Alternate Title
Disappearance of Mr. Davenheim, The	1923/03	Poirot	The Sketch	Mr. Davenby Disappears
Affair at the Victory Ball, The	1923/03	Poirot	The Sketch	
Jewel Robbery at the Grand Metropolitan	1923/03	Poirot	The Sketch	The Curious Disappearance of the Opalsen Pearls
King of Clubs, The	1923/03	Poirot	The Sketch	Beware the King of Clubs
Adventure of "The Western Star", The	1923/04	Poirot	The Sketch	
Plymouth Express, The	1923/04	Poirot	The Sketch	The Mystery of the Plymouth Express
Kidnapped Prime Minister, The	1923/04	Poirot	The Sketch	
Tragedy of Marsdon Manor, The	1923/04	Poirot	The Sketch	
While the Light Lasts	1923/04		Novel Magazine	
Million Dollar Bond Robbery, The	1923/05	Poirot	The Sketch	The Million Dollar Bank Robbery

Title	Earliest Date	Series Character	First Publication	Alternate Title
Mystery of Hunter's Lodge, The	1923/05	Poirot	The Sketch	
Adventure of the Cheap Flat, The	1923/05	Poirot	The Sketch	Poirot Indulges a Whim
Chocolate Box, The	1923/05	Poirot	The Sketch	The Clue of the Chocolate Box; The Time Hercule Poirot Failed
Actress, The	1923/05		Novel Magazine	A Trap For the Unwary
Adventure of the Egyptian Tomb, The	1923/09	Poirot	The Sketch	
Adventure of the Italian Nobleman, The	1923/10	Poirot	The Sketch	
Adventure of Johnny Waverly, The	1923/10	Poirot	The Sketch	The Kidnapping of Johnny Waverly
Market Basing Mystery, The	1923/10	Poirot	The Sketch	
Veiled Lady, The	1923/10	Poirot	The Sketch	
Case of the Missing Will, The	1923/10	Poirot	The Sketch	
Lost Mine, The	1923/11	Poirot	The Sketch	

Title	Earliest Date	Series Character	First Publication	Alternate Title
Submarine Plans, The	1923/11	Poirot	The Sketch	
Cornish Mystery, The	1923/11	Poirot	The Sketch	
Adventure of the Clapham Cook, The	1923/11	Poirot	The Sketch	The Mystery of the Clapham Cook
Adventure of the Christmas Pudding, version 1	1923/12	Poirot	The Sketch	Christmas Adventure
Lemeurier Inheritance, The	1923/12	Poirot	The Sketch	
Double Clue, The	1923/12	Poirot	The Sketch	The Dubious Clue
Clergyman's Daughter, The, and the Red House	1923/12	Tuppence & Tommy	Grand Magazine	The First Wish
In the House of the Enemy	1924/01	Poirot	The Sketch	
Radium Thieves, The	1924/01	Poirot	The Sketch	
Lady on the Stairs, The	1924/01	Poirot	The Sketch	The Woman on the Stairs
Adventure of the Dartmoor Bungalow, The	1924/01	Poirot	The Sketch	

Title	Earliest Date	Series Character	First Publication	Alternate Title
Unexpected Guest, The	1924/01	Poirot	The Sketch	
Baited Trap, The	1924/02	Poirot	The Sketch	
Chess Problem, A	1924/02	Poirot	The Sketch	
Yellow Jasmine Mystery, The	1924/02	Poirot	The Sketch	
Adventure of the Peroxide Blonde, The	1924/02	Poirot	The Sketch	
Girl in the Train, The	1924/02		Grand Magazine	
Dying Chinaman, The	1924/03	Poirot	The Sketch	
Terrible Catastrophe, The	1924/03	Poirot	The Sketch	
Crag in the Dolomites, The	1924/03	Poirot	The Sketch	
Coming of Mr. Quin, The	1924/03	Quin	Grand Magazine	The Passing of Mr. Quin
Red Signal, The	1924/06		Grand Magazine	

Title	Earliest Date	Series Character	First Publication	Alternate Title
Mystery of the Blue Jar, The	1924/07		Grand Magazine	
Jane in Search of a Job	1924/08		Grand Magazine	
Mr. Eastwood's Adventure	1924/08		Novel Magazine	The Mystery of the Second Cucumber, The Mystery of the Spanish Shawl
Pot of Tea, A	1924/09	Tuppence & Tommy	The Sketch	Publicity
Shadow on the Glass, The	1924/10	Quin	Grand Magazine	
Sunningdale Mystery, The	1924/10	Tuppence & Tommy	The Sketch	The Sunninghall Mystery
House of Lurking Death, The	1924/10	Tuppence & Tommy	Grand Magazine	
Case of The Missing Lady, The	1924/10	Tuppence & Tommy	The Sketch	The Disappearance of Mrs. Leigh Gordon
Affair of The Pink Pearl, The	1924/10	Tuppence & Tommy	The Sketch	
Finessing the King and the Gentleman Dressed in Newspaper	1924/10	Tuppence & Tommy	The Sketch	
Adventure of The Sinister Stranger, The	1924/10	Tuppence & Tommy	The Sketch	

Title	Earliest Date	Series Character	First Publication	Alternate Title
Blindman's Bluff	1924/11	Tuppence & Tommy	The Sketch	
Ambassador's Boots, The	1924/11	Tuppence & Tommy	The Sketch	
Crackler, The	1924/11	Tuppence & Tommy	The Sketch	The Affair of the Forged Notes
Philomel Cottage	1924/11		Grand Magazine	
Man Who Was No. 16, The	1924/12	Tuppence & Tommy	The Sketch	
Man in The Mist, The	1924/12	Tuppence & Tommy	The Sketch	
Manhood of Edward Robinson, The	1924/12		Grand Magazine	The Day of His Dreams
Witness for the Prosecution	1925/01		Flynn's Weekly	Traitor's Hands
Sign in the Sky, The	1925/07	Quin	Grand Magazine	
Within a Wall	1925/10		Royal Magazine	
At the Bells and Motley	1925/11	Quin	Grand Magazine	A Man of Magic

Title	Earliest Date	Series Character	First Publication	Alternate Title
Fourth Man, The	1925/12		Grand Magazine	
Listerdale Mystery	1925/12		Grand Magazine	The Benevolent Butler
Last Seance, The	1926		unknown	
House of Dreams, The	1926/01		Sovereign Magazine	House of Beauty
S.O.S.	1926/02		Grand Magazine	
Magnolia Blossom	1926/03		Royal Magazine	
Where There's a Will	1926/03		Mystery Magazine	Wireless
Rajah's Emerald	1926/07		Red Magazine	
Lonely God, The	1926/07		Royal Magazine	
Swan Song	1926/09		Grand Magazine	
Under Dog, The	1926/10	Poirot	London Magazine	

Title	Earliest Date	Series Character	First Publication	Alternate Title
Love Detectives	1926/10	Quin	Flynn's Weekly	At The Crossroads
Soul of the Croupier, The	1926/11	Quin	Flynn's Weekly	
World's End	1926/11	Quin	Flynn's Weekly	
Voice in the Dark, The	1926/12	Quin	Flynn's Weekly	
Edge, The	1927/02		Pearson's Magazine	
Harlequin's Lane	1927/05	Quin		The Storyteller
Tuesday Night Club, The	1927/12	Marple	Royal Magazine	
Motive vs. Opportunity	1928	Marple	Royal Magazine	
Ingots of Gold	1928	Marple	Royal Magazine	
Thumb Mark of Saint Peter	1928	Marple	Royal Magazine	
Herb of Death, The	1928	Marple	unknown	

Title	Earliest Date	Series Character	First Publication	Alternate Title
Blood-Stained Pavement, The	1928	Marple	Royal Magazine	
Idol House of Astarte	1928	Marple	Royal Magazine	
Wasp's Nest	1928/11	Poirot	The Daily Mail	The Worst of All
Unbreakable Alibi, The	1928/12	Tuppence & Tommy	Holly Leaves Magazine	
Accident	1929.		The Daily Express	
Next to a Dog	1929.		Grand Magazine	
Third Floor Flat	1929/01	Poirot	Detective Story Magazine	In the Third Floor Flat
Double Sin	1929/03	Poirot	Detective Story Magazine	By Road or Rail
Blue Geranium	1929/12	Marple	The Storyteller	
Man From the Sea, The	1930	Quin	Mysterious Mr. Quin	
Face of Helen, The	1930	Quin	Mysterious Mr. Quin	

Title	Earliest Date	Series Character	First Publication	Alternate Title
Dead Harlequin, The	1930	Quin	Mysterious Mr. Quin	
Bird with a Broken Wing	1930	Quin	Mysterious Mr. Quin	
Four Suspects, The	1930/01	Marple	Pictorial Review	
Christmas Tragedy, A	1930/01	Marple	The Storyteller	Never Two Without Three
Manx Gold	1930/05		London Daily Dispatch	
Companion, The	1932	Marple	Tuesday Club Murders	
Death By Drowning	1932	Marple	Tuesday Club Murders	
Affair at the Bungalow	1932	Marple	Tuesday Club Murders	
Case of the Discontented Soldier, The	1932	Pyne	Cosmopolitan	
Mystery of the Bagdad Chest, The	1932/01	Poirot	Strand Magazine	
Second Gong, The	1932/06	Poirot	Ladies Home Journal	

Title	Earliest Date	Series Character	First Publication	Alternate Title
Lamp, The	1933		Hound of Death	
Strange Case of Sir Arthur Carmichael, The	1933		Hound of Death	
Hound of Death, The	1933		Hound of Death	
Call of Wings, The	1933		Hound of Death	
Gipsy, The	1933		Hound of Death	
Have You Got Everything You Want?	1933/04	Pyne	Cosmopolitan	Express to Stamboul
Pearl of Price, The	1934	Pyne	Mr. Parker Pyne	
Oracle at Delphi, The	1934	Pyne	Mr. Parker Pyne	
House at Shiraz, The	1934	Pyne	Mr. Parker Pyne	
Gate of Baghdad, The	1934	Pyne	Mr. Parker Pyne	
Death on the Nile	1934	Pyne	Mr. Parker Pyne	

Title	Earliest Date	Series Character	First Publication	Alternate Title
Case of the Rich Woman, The	1934	Pyne	Mr. Parker Pyne	
Case of the Middle-Aged Wife, The	1934	Pyne	Mr. Parker Pyne	
Case of the Distressed Lady, The	1934	Pyne	Mr. Parker Pyne	
Case of the Discontented Husband, The	1934	Pyne	Mr. Parker Pyne	
Case of the City Clerk, The	1934	Pyne	Mr. Parker Pyne	
Golden Ball, The	1934		Listerdale Mystery	
Sing a Song of Sixpence	1934		Listerdale Mystery	
Fruitful Sunday, A	1934		Listerdale Mystery	
How Does Your Garden Grow?	1935/06	Poirot	Ladies Home Journal	
Problem at Sea	1935/12	Poirot	Strand Magazine	Poirot and the Crime in Cabin 66
Problem at Pollensa Bay	1936	Pyne	Strand Magazine	

Title	Earliest Date	Series Character	First Publication	Alternate Title
Regatta Mystery	1936	Pyne	Strand Magazine	
Triangle at Rhodes	1936/05	Poirot	Strand Magazine	
Incredible Theft, The	1937	Poirot	Dead Man's Mirror	
Dead Man's Mirror	1937	Poirot	Dead Man's Mirror	
Murder in the Mews	1937	Poirot	Dead Man's Mirror	
Yellow Iris	1937/07	Poirot	Strand Magazine	
Dream, The	1937/10	Poirot	The Saturday Evening Post	
Miss Marple Tells a Story	1939	Marple	Regatta Mystery	
In A Glass Darkly	1939		Regatta Mystery	
Horses of Diomedes	1940/06	Poirot	Strand Magazine	The Case of the Drug Peddler
Girdle of Hyppolita	1940/07	Poirot	Strand Magazine	The Disappearance of Winnie King

Title	Earliest Date	Series Character	First Publication	Alternate Title
Four and Twenty Blackbirds	1940/11	Poirot	Colliers	Poirot and the Regular Customer
Tape-Measure Murder	1942/02	Marple	Strand Magazine	The Case of the Retired Jeweller
Case of the Perfect Maid	1942/04	Marple	Strand Magazine	
Cretan Bull	1947	Poirot	Labours of Hercules	Midnight Madness
Ermanthian Boar	1947	Poirot	Labours of Hercules	Murder Mountain
Nemean Lion	1947	Poirot	Labours of Hercules	The Case of the Kidnapped Pekinese
Stymphalean Birds	1947	Poirot	Labours of Hercules	Birds of Ill Omen; The Vulture Women
Flock of Geryon	1947	Poirot	Labours of Hercules	Weird Monster
Apples of Hesperides	1947	Poirot	Labours of Hercules	The Poison Cup
Capture of Cerberus	1947	Poirot	Labours of Hercules	Meet Me In Hell
Arcadian Deer	1947	Poirot	Labours of Hercules	The Vanishing Lady

Title	Earliest Date	Series Character	First Publication	Alternate Title
Augean Stables	1947	Poirot	Labours of Hercules	
Lernean Hydra	1947	Poirot	Labours of Hercules	The Invisible Enemy
Case of the Caretaker	1950	Marple	Three Blind Mice	
Strange Jest	1950	Marple	Three Blind Mice	
Three Blind Mice	1950		Three Blind Mice	The Mousetrap
Sanctuary	1954/10	Marple	Women's Journal	
Greenshaw's Folly	1960/08	Marple	Women's Journal	
Dressmaker's Doll, The	1958		Women's Journal	
Mystery of the Spanish Chest	1960	Poirot	Adventure of the Christmas Pudding	
Theft of the Royal Ruby, The	1960	Poirot	Adventure of the Christmas Pudding	Adventure of the Christmas Pudding, version 2
Harlequin Tea Set, The	1971	Quin	Winter Crimes 3	

Appendix C

SHORT STORY COLLECTIONS

—Published during Agatha Christie's lifetime

Title	Alternate Title	Date	Character
Poirot Investigates		1924	Poirot
Partners in Crime		1929	Tuppence & Tommy
Mysterious Mr. Quin, The		1930	Harley Quin
Thirteen Problems	Tuesday Club Murders, The	1932	Marple
Hound of Death and Other Stories, The		1933	
Listerdale Mystery, The		1934	
Parker Pyne Investigates	Mr. Parker Pyne: Detective	1934	Parker Pyne
Murder in the Mews	Dead Man's Mirror	1937	
Regatta Mystery, The		1939	
Labours of Hercules, The		1947	Poirot

Title	Alternate Title	Date	Character
Labours of Hercules, The		1947	Poirot
Witness for the Prosecution		1948	
Three Blind Mice and Other Stories	Mousetrap and Other Stories, The	1950	
Under Dog and Other Mysteries, The		1951	
Adventure of the Christmas Pudding, The		1960	
Double Sin and Other Stories		1961	
13 for Luck!		1961	
Surprise! Surprise!		1965	
13 Clues for Miss Marple		1966	Marple
Golden Ball and Other Stories, The		1971	
Hercule Poirot's Early Cases		1974	Poirot
Harlequin Tea Set (published after Christie's death)		1989	

Bibliography

Christie, Agatha
Autobiography, An. Ballantine Books, New York, 1977.
Big Four, The. Dell Edition, New York, 1980.
Dead Man's Mirror. Berkley Edition, New York, 1984.
Double Sin and Other Stories. Berkley Edition, New York, 1984.
Golden Ball and Other Stories, The. Dell Edition, New York, 1982.
Harlequin Tea Set, The. G.P. Putnam Sons, New York, 1989.
Hercule Poirot's Casebook. Dodd, Mead & Co., New York, 1984.
Labors of Hercules, The. Dell Edition, New York, 1979.
Mr. Parker Pyne, Detective. Dell Edition, New York, 1957.
Mysterious Mr. Quin, The. Dell Edition, New York, 1977.
Partners in Crime. Berkley Edition, New York, 1984.
Poirot Investigates. Bantam Edition, New York, 1982.
Regatta Mystery, The. Dell Edition, New York, 1983.
Three Blind Mice and Other Stories. Berkley Edition, New York, 1984.
Tuesday Club Murders, The. Dell Edition, New York, 1982.
Under Dog and Other Stories, The. Dell Edition, New York, 1979.
Witness for the Prosecution, The. Berkley Edition, New York, 1986.

Godfrey, Thomas, ed.
Murder for Christmas. Mysterious Press, New York, 1982.

Riley and McAllister
New Bedside, Bathtub & Armchair Companion to Agatha Christie, The. Ungar Publishing, New York, 1979.

Wynne, Nancy Blue
Agatha Christie Chronology, An. Ace Books, New York, 1976.

Index

ELENA SANTANGELO is the author of the Possessed Mystery series, which includes Agatha Award finalist BY BLOOD POSSESSED and continues most recently with POISON TO PURGE MELANCHOLY. Sixteen of Elena's short stories have been published in the United States and Japan, and she served as co-editor of the short mystery anthology, Death Knell IV. You can contact her at www.elenasantangelo.com